COMBATANTS WILL BE DISPATCHED!
7
AF599237
"So, who am I supposed to incinerate?"
BELIAL
Known as Belial the Great Flame, a Supreme Leader of the Kisaragi Corporation. Has finally outgrown wearing cheap porn-actress costumes.
THIS VOLUME'S MAIN HEROINE
AGENT SIX'S VIEW
Why are you accentuating your breasts by using belts to give you extra cleavage? Why do you always have to make your clothes look so erotic?!

"Um, are your circuits shorting or something? That's Lady Belial before she got her enhancements."
THE THREE BACK IN THE DAY

"Hey, Six, who's this nervous-looking beauty standing next to Lady Lilith and Lady Astaroth?"

"What?! You wanna fight?! Fine, let's settle this!"
ROSE
AGENT SIX
BICKERING LIKE AN OLD MARRIED COUPLE...
AGENT SIX'S VIEW
Hey, stop that! You're about the same age! Try to be friends!

"RAAAAAAAA
AAAAAAAAA!"
LITTLE BASHIN

AGENT SIX'S VIEW
Get it together, Alice.
If we don't, he'll figure out...
ALICE KISARAGI
THIS IS COMBAT AGENT TEN

AGENT TEN
FRITZ
"Let me apologize for this unfortunate incident. With that said, we'd like to maintain the current arrangement if you are so willing."

CONTENTS

COMBATANTS WILL BE DISPATCHED

COMBATANTS WILL BE DISPATCHED!

7

Natsume Akatsuki

ILLUSTRATION BY

Kakao Lanthanum

COMBATANTS WILL BE DISPATCHED!

Natsume Akatsuki 7

Translation by Noboru Akimoto
Cover art by Kakao Lanthanum

This book is a work of fiction. Names, characters, places, and incidents are the product of the author's imagination or are used fictitiously. Any resemblance to actual events, locales, or persons, living or dead, is coincidental.

Yen On
150 West 30th Street, 19th Floor
New York, NY 10001

Visit us at yenpress.com
facebook.com/yenpress
twitter.com/yenpress
yenpress.tumblr.com
instagram.com/yenpress

First Yen On Edition: October 2023

Edited by Yen On Editorial: Payton Campbell, Maya Deutsch
Designed by Yen Press Design: Eddy Mingki

Yen On is an imprint of Yen Press, LLC.
The Yen On name and logo are trademarks of Yen Press, LLC.

The publisher is not responsible for websites (or their content) that are not owned by the publisher.

Library of Congress Cataloging-in-Publication Data
Names: Akatsuki, Natsume, author. | Lanthanum, Kakao, illustrator. | Akimoto, Noboru, translator.
Title: Combatants will be dispatched! / Natsume Akatsuki ; illustration by Kakao Lanthanum ; translation by Noboru Akimoto ; cover art by Kakao Lanthanum.
Other titles: Sentoin haken shimasu!. English
Description: First Yen On edition. | New York : Yen On, 2019.
Identifiers: LCCN 2019025056 | ISBN 9781975385583 (v. 1 ; trade paperback) | ISBN 9781975331528 (v. 2 ; trade paperback) | ISBN 9781975399023 (v. 3 ; trade paperback) | ISBN 9781975313685 (v. 4 ; trade paperback) | ISBN 9781975316556 (v. 5 ; trade paperback) | ISBN 9781975325169 (v. 6 ; trade paperback) | ISBN 9781975367664 (v. 7 ; trade paperback)
Subjects: CYAC: Science fiction. | Robots—Fiction.
Classification: LCC PZ7.1.A38 Se 2019 | DDC [Fic]—dc23
LC record available at https://lccn.loc.gov/2019025056

ISBNs: 978-1-9753-6766-4 (paperback)
978-1-9753-6767-1 (ebook)

10 9 8 7 6 5 4 3 2 1

LSC-C

Printed in the United States of America

Prologue

After barging into my room unannounced, Alice begins rooting around my belongings and speaks up after flipping through a photo album.

"Hey, Six, who's this nervous-looking beauty standing next to Lady Lilith and Lady Astaroth? I can't find her in my database."

I peer over her shoulder at the picture in question to see who she's talking about, and I'm greeted by the image of a beautiful woman sandwiched between Lilith and Astaroth, smiling shyly at the camera as though she's shrinking back from it.

The photo's from back when I first joined Kisaragi, when the beauty in question intervened to smooth things over after Astaroth and Lilith had gone at it with hammers and tongs.

Though gorgeous, the woman in question always tended to hunch forward because she was uncomfortable with her own height.

"Um, are your circuits shorting or something? That's Lady Belial before she got her enhancements."

At my comment, Alice does a double-take and looks at the photo a second time.

"...This black-haired, cultured-looking chick is the same person as Lady Belial, the redheaded bombshell?"

In the photo Belial is dressed in a plain white kimono.

Then again, in the same picture, Astaroth's wearing a skirt and suit like some office lady, while Lilith's wearing a regular school uniform.

Astaroth is making no effort at concealing her displeasure, while Lilith is rigidly facing the camera, a serious look on her face.

"Yup. Before she got modded, Lady Belial was the most normal person in all of Kisaragi. She was kind and well-mannered yet weirdly erotic, and I went out of my way to tease her whenever I had the chance."

"You sexually harassed a gentle-looking person like her?" asks Alice with a note of exasperation as I think back to how Belial used to be.

"At the time, Lady Belial lacked a lot of confidence despite the fact that she was pretty much the best fighter out of all of us. She was also smart as a whip and had a banging body. I only harassed with the best of intentions, to get her to understand she had a lot to offer."

"Whatever the intentions, sexual harassment is still sexual harassment, you idiot. God, what an asshole."

Because she lacked confidence in herself, Belial was skeptical that others found her attractive, so she tended to leave herself open a lot of the time.

I didn't *want* to do it, but I knew that *someone* had to sexually harass her to make sure she wouldn't be caught off guard by someone with sinister motives.

Then again, looking back, it sometimes felt like she left herself vulnerable to me on purpose, as though she was *hoping* I'd one day act on my advances. The things I said never really seemed to bother her that much.

"Still, how the hell did this woman end up like the current Lady Belial? Didn't Lady Lilith do the enhancement surgery herself?"

Seems Lilith hadn't installed that bit of data into Alice's brain.

"Yeah, that's right. Lady Lilith handled the surgery… Hey, you know why Lady Belial's the most powerful person in Kisaragi?"

"It's because of her amazing pyrokinesis powers that she earned the title of 'the Incinerator,' right? I've also heard she's had the most enhancement surgeries of any of the combatants in all of Kisaragi."

Kisaragi's been enhancing its soldiers through superpowers gained through brain surgery for a while now, and Belial's biggest asset is the pyrokinesis she gained from that procedure.

When Lilith told Belial that the amount of power gained from the surgery was correlated with the amount of brain capacity devoted to that ability, Belial didn't hesitate for a moment in choosing to maximize her power.

As a result, Lilith pushed the limits of just how far she could take the surgery without impacting Belial's personality, memories, or ability to function, but…

"Lady Lilith screwed up. When the other researchers checked in on what happened, it seemed she'd gone way past the line that shouldn't be crossed when modifying Lady Belial's brain."

"Of course she did."

That was a hell of a time. I had to talk Astaroth down from executing Lilith, calm the mutants that wanted to kill Lilith, and stop the Combat Agents who wanted to string Lilith up on a light pole.

"Lady Lilith insisted that she'd been careful not to cross the line and that someone else had messed up the settings, but everyone was a hair's breadth from snapping at her because of her attitude. That's when Lady Belial stepped in and told us that it was fine, or rather that it was exactly what she wanted."

"Isn't Lady Lilith the way she is now because Lady Belial wouldn't give her a kick in the ass when she needed it?"

It was an egregious case of malpractice, but given that Belial herself seemed fine with it, Lilith is just about the only one who's still bothered by the outcome. However…

"Seemed Lady Lilith did feel kind of guilty about it, so she's still trying to restore Lady Belial's memories. She's tried things like showing Lady Belial old videos and pissing her off or delivering a strong blow to Lady Belial's head to jog her brain, only to get smacked in return."

"Obviously, she's not actually trying to fix her. Still, must've been a hell of a thing to deal with, partner. I don't know anything about what things were like at the time, but Lady Belial's now the definition of a loose cannon. Based on the photo, it looks like she was the gentle type—right up your alley," Alice says teasingly as she looks over the picture.

I mean, it's true, I did love the Belial who was kind, a little shy, and interested in erotic things but went out of her way to pretend she didn't enjoy my lewd advances, although…

…I'm pretty fond of the current Belial, who's basically an uncontrollable force of nature, too.

CHAPTER 1

Hiiragi Attacks

1

After settling our differences with the Kisaragi Corporation's second-rate imitation, aka, the Hiiragi Agency of Order, the Torace Kingdom was renamed, becoming the Hiiragi-Torace territory.

From our point of view, we basically had Torace nabbed out from under us by a newcomer, but we've managed to secretly link the capital of Torace to our Hideout City with a subterranean tunnel, and we're currently mining large amounts of water crystals every day.

Because it's possible they'll find out we're illegally mining the water crystals, we've decided not to worry about saturating the market and are selling the crystals as quickly as we mine them.

Our competition seemed perplexed by the sudden glut in water crystals, but for now, it looks like they've decided to just watch how the market shakes out before resuming their own mining operations.

Torace has always been a wealthy country with plenty of money, so they have the resources to be able to sit back and let their laborers rest while keeping an eye on water crystal prices.

Which fits perfectly with our plans to make money from the gems while we still have access to them.

Basically, there aren't any major issues at the moment, and we're making good progress on our local invasion preparations…

I sit in Viper's office, lit softly by the afternoon sun, and listen to the sounds of her pen scratching across the surface of her paperwork and the gentle snoring coming from Rose, curled up at her feet.

As we hang out, Grimm softly says, "How peaceful…"

Viper's pen pauses at Grimm's remark.

"Yes, indeed. It's a lovely calm. None of our Combat Agents need to be exposed to danger and…"

Viper smiles over at sleepy-eyed Grimm.

"Tsk tsk… Still trying to play the good girl, hmm? Have you forgotten that you're supposed to be part of the leadership of an evil corporation…? The whole reason they keep Combat Agents around is to fight! A peaceful period is nothing to celebrate."

"Oh! Y-you're right, of course. I shouldn't be glad for peace. Um… The Bashin tribe reported that they encountered a new monster in the woods. I'll go and investigate. Depending on what I find, could be some fresh conflict, so…"

"How can you be so confidently wrong?! You're supposed to be management! You need to be making use of your underlings! Take a page from the Grace Kingdom's old chief of staff. That rotten pig kept sending Rose and me into the heart of the most intense fighting. You need to learn to start abusing your underlings a bit more and make them do things they don't want to do!"

In a rare role reversal, Grimm's the one making sense as Viper basks in the tranquil atmosphere of her office.

"Things they don't want to do…"

Trying to think of things her subordinates might not want to do, Viper looks over in my direction.

"Mr. Six, you seem to have time on your hands. Could you please help me organize my paperwork?"

"I may look like I'm not doing much, but I'm actually super busy. And Vi, while I admire your desire to become a proper evil leader, you shouldn't be offloading your work onto others."

"Y-yes, you're completely right! M-my apologies."

"Hold on there! You can't just give up like that! Look at him more carefully. He's clearly slacking off! Commander, tell the class what you're actually doing!"

Grimm's screeching interrupts Viper as she tries to resume working.

I show off the magnifying glass in my hand and point to the blue water crystal sitting on a plate.

"Water crystals slowly melt into water when you warm them up. I'm watching a crystal melt because it looks pretty cool."

"See! He's not busy at all! If you're that bored, head off to Grunade already!"

There's a country called Grunade.

In the deepest parts of what used to be the Demon Lord's realm, there's a mountain range called the Midgard Mountains, and Grunade considers it holy terrain.

The country rests at the foot of the Midgard Mountains and is also a big center of dragon worship, since its people still believe that ancient dragons watch over them.

And…

"…Grunade's all up in a stir because a mysterious monster stole their sorcery stone, right? It'd be pretty rude to visit them while they're dealing with that, don't you think?"

They're in quite a mess because the sorcery stone that's their national treasure was stolen.

"…Hey, Commander, it's time to face reality, yes? I'm sure by now even you've realized who actually stole the sorcery stone," Grimm says with an exasperated sigh. But if I admit this, it'll turn a minor problem into a major diplomatic incident.

Even though we're planning to eventually invade Grunade, now isn't the right time to go around making new enemies since we just finished settling a cease-fire with our imitators.

After all, we're busy mining water crystals from right under their noses. Once they figure out what we've been doing, we can kiss this armistice goodbye.

"Now, let's not be hasty, Grimm. You all seem eager to pass judgment on Tiger Man, but so far it's just circumstantial evidence!"

"Do you really think there's another feline monster who walks on two legs and goes around purring and meowing?"

She's got me there, but the moment I accept that she's right, I lose.

"I know of other feline monsters that could steal a national treasure. The group we fought the other day had a giant cat as a pet, remember?"

"I said walks on two legs! Don't try covering your ears to deny it! Look at me!"

I resist Grimm's efforts at persuasion by plugging my ears, even as she grabs me by the shoulders and shakes me back and forth.

"Mmph. Grimm, what are you shouting about…? It's midday, shouldn't you be asleep…?"

Rose, who's been napping at Viper's feet, sits up, rubbing the sleep out of her eyes.

"Why am I, the nocturnal one, actually working while you're taking a nap?! …Speaking of which, Rose, you've gotten a lot more dog-like lately," Grimm says with a note of exasperation, prompting Rose to leap to her feet.

"You may be my friend, Grimm, but comparing me to a mutt is going too far! And if that's what you're calling me, then I'll just say it! Lately you've been acting like an old lady, napping all day in the shade!"

"My my, you've got a mouth on you, don't you, young lady? Fine. I'll inflict you with a curse as big as the one I put on the entire country of Torace!"

"C-calm down, please, both of you…"

The pair instantly enters combat mode, and Viper, caught between the two of them, shoots me a pleading gaze.

I avoid looking in their direction and continue lighting the crystal with my magnifying glass.

"It's so peaceful…"

"It's not peaceful at all! Help me defuse this, Mr. Six!"

The Kisaragi Corporation's Local Branch is currently enjoying a blissful lull in the action.

2

To avoid the unfolding chaos in Viper's room, I decide to kill time by wandering around Hideout City when I come upon a surprising sight.

"Miss Snow, thank you so much! You were a great help!"

"Think nothing of it. Call me if you ever need help. I'll come as soon as I can."

A hardhat-clad Snow dismounts an excavator at a construction site as the demons around her offer thanks.

…Why is a local like her operating construction equipment?

"Hey, what are you doing? You can't just go driving our heavy machinery around."

"What are you babbling about this time? I have a license to operate this thing."

She then holds out a license.

"Why does a local like you have one of these?!"

"Alice printed it for me. If you listen to her lecture, then pass the operator's exam, she'll issue one for you, too. This isn't the only certification I've picked up, either. I've passed a bunch of other exams as well. After all, every new certification means a bump in salary!"

Unbelievable. Her license shows that she's got more certifications than I do.

...That's right—Snow is a former street urchin who worked her way into becoming a knight commander by hauling herself up by her bootstraps.

"...What are you doing back here anyway? Weren't you hyped about reclaiming your knighthood or something?"

Yes, her recent achievements were enough to get her reinstated...

"Her Highness told me to cooperate with Kisaragi as a part-timer, because that would allow me to deepen the Kingdom's ties to Kisaragi while earning money and learning about your technology. Thanks to that, I'm in the wonderful position of earning salaries from both the kingdom *and* Kisaragi!"

"Hey, that's not fair! You collect two checks?!"

So now Snow's learning the ins and outs of Kisaragi tech... Isn't that like spying?!

She's essentially earning a double salary to be a double agent. Are you kidding me...?

"It's not much different than when you were getting paid by the kingdom to be a knight while serving as a spy for Kisaragi."

"Uh-huh...well, anyway, where's Alice? I needed to talk to her about Tiger Man."

"Don't try to change the subject."

Even as she interjects, Snow nods at my question.

"Alice is over there trying to reeducate the former leaders of the Demon Lord Army, but... It's probably easier to just show you than try to explain. Alice is acting a bit strangely. Her usual cold logic is nowhere to be found. See if you can do something for her."

Snow deliberately keeps her description vague and points to a building in front of her.

* * *

It's a school building constructed for the education of demon children.

In addition to teaching the typical subjects, the school also plays up how wonderful an organization the Kisaragi Corporation is, in the hopes that they'll be brainwashed—er, educated—to become obedient workers in the future.

The curriculum has been adjusted to match the local conditions, and it includes a smattering of reading, writing, and arithmetic; lectures on the glorious history of the Kisaragi Corporation; lessons on how to recognize and deal with the threat of local wildlife; and ways to recognize and gather the most valuable resources in the area.

I guess their class is out today. I don't see any kids around, but I do hear familiar voices echoing from one of the classrooms.

"Again, how did you arrive at that answer?! You started out so well!"

"Don't look at me! Alice, you're the one who's going off on weird tangents!"

"Heine's right! I was following along just fine until the middle part! Then you suddenly lost me!"

I follow the voices and peer into the classroom. There, I see Alice standing at the lectern, engaged in an argument with Heine and Russell.

Catching sight of me through the hallway window, Alice gestures for me to enter and join them.

"Oh, good timing, Six. A question for a veteran agent like you. Let's say you're ordered to take fifty agents and wipe out an enemy base. It's expected to take you two weeks. How much are you going to prepare in terms of supplies?"

…Basic math problem?

I guess the reasoning that I can bring down the base in three days isn't going to cut it here.

"Given there's the possibility our advance could be slowed by bad

weather and the chance that enemy resistance might be greater than expected, I'd say three weeks' worth of rations and ammo for fifty agents… Hey! Why are you patting my head?"

"It's just nice to know that even though your brain's usually just for show, it still works when it comes to combat operations."

…Was that a compliment or an insult?

Alice continues to pat my head affectionately, then turns to Heine.

"Let's say we gave Heine fifty orcs and ordered her to use them to take out a Hiiragi base. Let's also assume it'll take a week to eliminate the fortress… Well, Heine? What sorts of supplies would you prepare?"

"I'd prepare fifty acorns to give the orcs when they finish."

"All right, starting today, you're now officially dumber than Six."

"Why?! There's nothing wrong with my answer!"

Should I interrupt Alice, who's using me as the standard of stupidity, or comment on Heine's silly answer?

While Heine panics over Alice's evaluation of her answer, Russell confidently steps up to bat.

"I get it, now. Listen, Heine, it's not like you have to give them the acorns at the start of the battle. You can always give them the acorns when you get back. Which means you can go without carrying any supplies at all."

"Okay, you're also on the dumber-than-Six list, Russell. Go join Rose and work on some simple addition and subtraction problems."

"Wait! I'm not like my cousin! I can do math! I mean, I was one of the Elite Four!"

Alice gives the frustrated Russell an exasperated look.

"Right, that's exactly what I'm trying to get across to you. Kisaragi's Combat Agents all tend to be too self-centered and selfish to make effective commanders. If you can actually lead units, you'll spend less time at the power plant. So quit screwing around and take this seriously!"

"We *are* taking this seriously!"

"That's right! You're the one who's being weird here, Alice! You need to explain what's wrong with our answers!"

I thought they were some of the smarter ones, at least by Kisaragi standards.

"...Fine. First, you're not properly calculating the necessary rations based on the unit size and mission length. Also, forget about the acorns."

Heine crinkles her brow in thought, struggling with the premise of Alice's question.

"Food for fifty orc soldiers? Um, how would you even calculate that? They'll just keep eating so long as there's anything edible on hand."

"Why do we need to carry rations at all given that orcs can fatten up and go without food for a whole month? I mean, those supplies would just slow down the march."

Alice freezes at Russell's words as the two former Demon Lord Army commanders discuss the question.

"Wait, repeat what you just said. You're saying that if they eat enough, orcs can be active for an entire month without extra food?"

"Yeah, though if they fatten up too much, they get sluggish. Wild orcs gain weight in autumn, then go hibernate in subterranean lairs during winter when food is scarce. Of course, the monsters are also starving in winter. So a fair number of orc lairs get dug up, and some hibernating orcs get eaten."

Ah, another one of the harsh realities of living in a world infested by monsters. No wonder orcs want to live and work on human farms.

I get it now. I can see why these two are having trouble understanding what Alice was asking.

From the look on Heine and Russell's faces, it seems they've also figured out what Alice's mistake was.

"Since the Demon Lord's lands are mostly desert, we were always facing food shortages, so whenever we went on the offensive, we lived off the land… Acorns were usually a good-enough reward."

"How the hell am I supposed to know about your food scarcity or ecology?! I'm gonna throw acorns at *you*, dammit!"

As Russell shrinks from Alice's threats, I remember something.

"Didn't you guys have supply companies when you were leading armies for the Demon Lord? The first time I ran into Heine, it was when we were burning a supply train."

That's right, we were ruthlessly attacking a supply train at the time, and Heine came to stop us…

"Oh, that was grub for the goblin troops. Unlike orcs, who can store fat, or ogres, who only eat what they've killed themselves, goblins will eat just about anything. They'll even start eating each other if they get too hungry."

"Stop! If you say any more, I'll have to start thinking of the goblin civilians in town as potential cannibals!"

Aaand there's another piece of demon trivia that I would have been better off not knowing…like the orc farms.

"Hey, Alice. Are we done with the lectures? I mean, I commanded troops for the Demon Lord Army countless times. There shouldn't be a problem with me doing it again… So why don't we go and pick him up?"

Russell pretends to speak casually as he looks off into the distance.

"Who are you talking about? Hideout City is in the middle of a massive construction boom. We can't exactly afford to divert resources to nonvital tasks since we're short on manpower as it is."

"You know who I'm talking about! Yeah, he's kind of creepy, and all of his meowing and purring gets annoying, but don't we need him? I mean, isn't he the strongest out of all of you?"

Of course, the "he" Russell is talking about must be Tiger Man. I guess the fact that Tiger Man has forced Russell to cross-dress, used him as a body pillow, hiked up his skirt, and subjected him to all sorts of other harassment makes Russell hesitant to even use his name.

"You too, Russell? You think Tiger Man's the one who stole Grunade's national treasure? I can't believe you're finger pointing without proof. Tsk, tsk."

"Who else could have done it?!"

Alice rests her hand on Russell's head to try to calm the surprisingly vehement chimera.

"Hey, Russell, the only thing we know for sure at this moment is that a large feline monster stole a sorcery stone belonging to a country called Grunade, which has thrown everything into chaos over there… And not to change the subject, but an organization we recently skirmished with had a giant feline monster as a pet."

Grasping what Alice is hinting at, Russell stares at her in disbelief.

"…A-are you planning to frame Hiiragi for the theft?!"

"Frame? No one said anything about framing. I'm just stating facts. The only orgs known to have feline monsters as pets are us and Hiiragi. And there's no hard evidence that paints Tiger Man as the culprit. So what we need to do in this situation is have faith in our comrade Tiger Man. Isn't that right, Six?"

"Yep, I believe in Tiger Man. Kisaragi values its people. Hey, Russell, when did you become so jaded?"

Russell's jaw drops at that.

"W-wait, wait, wait! Why are you making it sound like I'm the bad guy here?! I mean, sure, I value my friends and comrades, too! But based on motives and circumstances…"

Alice gently pats Russell's head.

"When it comes to villainy, the important stuff happens once the hard evidence starts coming out. It's too early to panic. Isn't that right, Six?"

"Yeah. When the evidence is this thin, it's best to point to the shortcomings in the accusers' case and act like we're being victimized by them. Then when the accusers briefly back down, they're met with an unfortunate little accident."

"W-wow… This is why humans are…"

Heine looks at a loss for words as Russell pushes Alice's hand off his head.

"…H-hey, Russell? Don't you hate that beastman? I mean, you do nothing but complain about him, so I figured you'd be happy he was out for a bit…"

Russell harumphs in exasperation and looks coldly over at Heine.

"…*Of course* I hate him, and I'm glad he's not here! But I do know that he's powerful, and chimeras obey strong creatures out of instinct."

Seems this is the first time she's had a colleague look at her that way. Heine appears uncomfortable as she responds.

"I-I see! Okay, if you say so! I'm glad to hear it. Y'know, you had me worried a bit because you squealed like a girl when Six flipped up your skirt the other day."

"…D-did I really sound like a girl?" Russell asks in shock as Heine glances away.

Alice then addresses the pair of them:

"Now that the Grace Kingdom's absorbed the Demon Lord's territories, Grace and Grunade share a border. Besides, Princess Tillis has already taken the initiative and sent them a letter saying, 'We're pleased to have you as a neighbor. As a neighborly warning, our kingdom was recently attacked by a giant feline monster owned by the Hiiragi Agency of Order. We hope you haven't been similarly attacked.'"

"You know, there's a line that you shouldn't cross, even against your enemies. Honestly you guys are worse than us demons."

"Yep, humanity definitely needs to go extinct."

I'll take that as a compliment.

3

Construction in Hideout City continues even as we wait for a response to Tillis's diplomatic letter and emissary.

We send over samples of monsters from the forest and newly discovered resources, receiving supplies and materials of equal value in return.

Because we spare no expense and instantly spend the resources we've received, the population is booming from people flocking to Hideout City in search of food and job opportunities.

Now all we have to do is finish clearing the forest and begin working on agricultural and industrial districts.

Alice is currently figuring out how to deal with the hostile creatures like the alraunes that guard the forest, so it should only be a matter of time before we get to that stage of development.

...I ponder such things as I slack off while pretending to keep watch on the observation platform. Just then, I see a visitor approaching the city limits.

It's Little Bashin, a young girl bearing tribal markings and a hand ax. For some reason, Rose regards her as a rival.

"...! ...!"

When Little Bashin notices me on the observation platform, she waves enthusiastically.

She started coming to visit regularly ever since I gave her the ax, which I procured from Earth. Despite her primal appearance, she's quite reasonable at heart and very polite, so the people of Hideout City are happy to continue welcoming her as a visitor.

"Drown in a sea of hellfire... Sleep for all eternity! Crimson Breeeeath!"

"?!"

Suddenly, a gout of flame erupts toward the welcomed visitor.

Although she manages to avoid a direct hit, the flames ignite her clothing and Little Bashin rolls onto the ground to put out the fire.

"—!! —!!!"

"Did you think you could come into my territory and leave unscathed? It's time to settle this once and for all— Ow!"

After hopping off the observation tower, I smack Rose upside the head.

"What was that for, Boss?! This girl's an enemy of Kisaragi!"

"You're the only one who thinks of her that way. Seriously, you gotta stop attacking Little Bashin every time she comes to play. We're trying to build friendly relations with her tribe."

The Bashin are rather civilized people despite their primitive appearances, but they're extremely adept at fighting in the woods.

And since our woodlands combat expert, Tiger Man, is off doing who knows what, it's a bad idea to make an enemy of them.

...After putting out her burning clothes, Little Bashin hops back onto her feet, ax in hand.

"Raaaaaaaaaaaaaaaaaaaaaaaaa!!"

"What, you wanna fight?! Fine, let's settle this!"

"Hey, stop that! You're around the same age! Try to be friends!"

Little Bashin stares down Rose, seemingly ready to pounce, but then she slowly approaches with an almost pleading gesture and hands me a letter.

Since I can't read the local language, I hand it to Rose.

"Umm... 'To the Honored Members of the Kisaragi Corporations. Greetings. It is our hope that this letter, written in the days when the Deadplanters are emitting the sweet fragrances from their blossoms, finds you all in good health and fortune. We, the Bashin tribe, as a warrior clan that respects both martial prowess and honor, would like to express our heartfelt admiration of your company's glorious record in battle, and your compassionate and honorable behavior in welcoming the refugees of the Demon Lord realms, your former enemies, into your arms.'"

Given the way the language sounds when spoken, I can't help but wonder if that's really what's written in the letter...

"...Is that really what's written there?"

"Um, the words are kind of hard for me to understand, but yeah, that's what it says, Boss."

Rose looks up at me a bit quizzically before she resumes reading.

"'In addition to expressing our admiration, we wish to ask a favor of you, in spite of our knowledge that such a thing would be an imposition. It is our desire to discuss the terms under which we could send our children to your settlement to shelter among your people. While we are loath to go into specifics on such a personal matter, we have been in a long-standing feud with the Hiiragi tribe. However, they have recently acquired strange new, unnatural tools that allow them to command large monsters, including those that belong to the dragon family. Consequently, we find ourselves at a disadvantage. Our children, though young, are still members of the Bashin tribe, and we believe they would still be of great use to you in the woods. We understand that you have much business to attend to, but we would be gratified if you could be so kind as to respond to our missive. We have the honor of being your most humble, obedient servants.'"

Goddammit, they're better letter writers than I am!

Upon closer inspection, I see that Little Bashin is covered in small cuts and bruises.

While a part of me wonders if they were the result of her little horseplay with Rose, the scratches look like claw marks from monsters.

I climb back to the top of the observation platform and yell into the loudspeaker.

"All hands on deck!"

The Combat Agents in the conference room voice their displeasure at the sudden summons.

"What now, Six? We're busy as hell. We're close to finishing up the apartments in the residential district today. Get on with whatever you want and let us get back to work."

"We know you're bored out of your tiny little mind, but we've got work to do, dammit. We need to at least get shelter ready for the residents before winter…"

"This planet doesn't get much rain, so I don't think there'll be a lot of snow, but we still need to hurry."

Seems my colleagues have been so busy with their construction work that they've forgotten who they're supposed to be.

"Get a load of you guys! A bunch of henchmen learning the joys of honest work?! HAH! You've all gone softer than melted cheese! Do you even remember what your *real* jobs are?"

"W-w-we're well aware of our real jobs! I admit, it was pretty fun to have the demons cheering us on, but we haven't gone soft, dammit!"

"Considering we've always been sent to harass people, it's nice to be appreciated for once! Anyway, if you're gonna talk that much shit, you better have some combat work for us!"

"If that's what you want, then I've got good news. There's trouble," says Alice.

Her unexpected words rouse the defanged Combat Agents.

"Oh, really? A combat mission?"

"Why didn't you just say so?! Screw construction work!"

"We'll show you we haven't gone soft!"

Now that their Combat Agent instincts have kicked in, they're dripping with an obnoxious amount of bravado.

"The Bashin Warrior tribe are losing their turf war, so they want us to at least go and offer their kids protection."

The agents all sober up and put on their most serious expressions at Alice's explanation.

"Despite appearances, the Bashins have always been good neighbors. I've got no complaints about going to secure their children, but…

Our main job is to deploy as Combat Agents! You guys know what you gotta do!"

"Yep!" shout the agents, motivated at last.

Alice nods with satisfaction.

"That's what I like to hear! Hiiragi agents are using strange devices to control dragons and giant monsters, but…Kisaragi is the strongest there is! Now's the time to show them who we really are!"

"""""…Uhh, yeah…"""""

Suddenly much less boisterous, my colleagues can only muster a ragged cheer.

4

"Hey, Boss, there's a supopocchi lying over there! Seems like we're in Bashin tribe territory! Since we're here, why don't we take it home with us?"

"It's not just lying there. The Bashins impaled it on the tree branch to dry it out."

The cheerful, hungry chimera leads our group as we trek into the dangerous depths of the woods.

Rose isn't the only one who's in a good mood.

"Finally, our time to shine! Demons live to fight! I'll show 'em what an elite soldier of a demon lord's army can do!"

"The whole maid bit was starting to mess with my head a little. Time to get back to what a combat chimera was made to do. Sorry, Heine, but I'll be taking most of the glory on the battlefield."

The POWs who are usually employed as green electricity generators also sound enthused, eager to take out their pent-up frustration on the enemy.

And…

"We live to fight, too! After all, it's even in our names! We're Combat Agents!"

"Busty and Rusty can wait in the back. Don't get in our way!"

"There was talk of dragons, but a lizard's a lizard at the end of the day. I'll admit, I was scared when I first heard about 'em, but they're a damned sight less scary than the giant robots the capes use!"

My colleagues also puff out their chests, resigned to fighting dragons and unwilling to let the locals have all the glory.

"D-did you just call me 'Busty'?" asks Heine.

"Could you not call me 'Rusty,' please?" Russell adds.

Since this is our first combat operation in a while, we've got a lot of people eager for blood in our little party.

It's me in the lead, two combat chimeras, the booby slave, and three expendable Combat Agents.

"Hey, Six, given that she's throwing us into this meat grinder, where the hell did Alice get off to?"

"I mean, she has her problems, but at least she's sharp. It's a little unnerving thinking you're in charge down here."

"Look at the party composition, man. It's four dudes and three girls. I mean, sure, Alice is an android, but if she were here, it'd at least be fifty-fifty. C'mon, man, *think* before you let her walk off like that."

The expendables complain about Alice's absence.

"This is a recon-in-force mission to check in on the giant monsters and the Hiiragi tribe. There's no need to bring Alice. She's busy enough as it is building up Hideout City. Leave the rough jobs to me."

"Um...why am I being considered a girl for the count?" asks the cross-dressing chimera with a troubled look, but no one responds to his comment.

Just then:

"Something smells good. Boss, are you getting a whiff of it, too? What a delicious aroma...like roasting meat..."

Rose, leading the charge, sniffs hungrily at the air.

I guess combat chimeras have a sharp sense of smell. Russell is also sniffing frantically…

"Yeah, something's burning. It's a pretty nice aroma… No, wait, this smell!"

He takes off toward the scent.

"Russell, what's going on?! Don't go off on your own—it's dangerous!"

"Don't try to claim it all for yourself! If there's feral meat out there, we should split it!"

"I'm not just gonna eat something I found lying around. And what the heck is feral meat anyway? Heine, this smell… It's Isaac! Isaac is burning! The scent's coming from just up ahead!"

We follow Russell to a small clearing in the woods where a griffin with wounds all over its body lies resting.

"Isaaaac!" screams Heine with tears in her eyes as she rushes to the griffin's side.

"Miss Heine, you can't just name it to try to claim ownership! I want the thigh meat!"

"You idiot! Isaac is my pet! He's not for eating!"

Heine clings to the griffin, then tries to shield it from Rose with her back.

"Oh, right, I forgot you used to ride a griffin. I was wondering what happened to it. I guess you were keeping it out here?"

"I couldn't do anything about being taken captive, but I didn't want to drag Isaac into it, so I let him go free. Griffins are strong, so I figured he'd be fine out in the woods. But…it seems I was wrong. Oh, Isaac, I'm so sorry…"

As Heine weeps, Rose continues to eye Isaac as if he's a roast chicken.

"Hey, if Isaac was released into the woods, that means he doesn't belong to anyone, right?"

"...R-Rose, l-let me just note that griffins don't taste very good. If you try to eat Isaac under these circumstances, I'm gonna find it hard to keep thinking of you as a cousin."

Russell's face twitches as he holds his hands out to Isaac and chants.

"You know, I chewed on Isaac a little when I fought Heine back in the day, but I'm pretty sure I didn't like the taste because there wasn't any seasoning. But he smells amazing right now... I think I could really warm up to it."

"Stop it! Get away from him! Russell, hurry up and heal him!"

As Heine desperately shields Isaac, Russell's hands begin glowing.

"Oh, cool. Water magic having healing properties is totally a fantasy trope. Hey, Rusty, I ended up getting a certain something caught in my zipper earlier. Think you can you heal that?"

"Rusty is both adorable and can use magic, as for the other chimera...*sigh...*"

"What about me, huh? Depending on what you were about to say, I may change my mind and eat you instead!"

"Could you guys shut up for a second? I need quiet to concentrate!"

They're making a scene in front of the griffin, but do they understand what's actually happening here?

The fact that Isaac's lying there with burns means that the one who gave it those wounds should still be nearby...

"...? Hey, it's gone dark all of a—"

Heine looks up at the sky and falls silent.

Seeing her reaction, the expendable Combat Agents do the same and brandish their weapons.

As the sun is eclipsed by something above us and a darkness envelops our little party, I throw a flash bang into the air—

"Raaaaagh! Take that!"

A dragon, the most powerful lifeform on this planet, dives toward us, but the flash bang explodes in a cacophony of noise and light. The creature plummets to the ground, its eyes damaged.

"G-g-g-good job, Six! Nice use of your vast experience!"

"U-using a stun grenade to bring down a dragon in the air is common sense for anyone who plays *MonPan*! In the end, dragons are just giant lizards! Hah!"

"Bwah-ha-ha! Taste modern firepower, savage beast! Now's our chance—get 'em!"

I don't mind watching expendables get excited by my achievement.

"Sheesh, all I did was throw a grenade… Hey Rose, did you see how awesome your commander—"

"Gaaaaah!"

The three locals who were gazing up at the sky are all clawing at their blinded eyes.

"Screeeee!"

Then the dragon, having crashed into the ground, suddenly begins to thrash about wildly in a blind fury, cutting down the trees around it.

"Ack! S-Six, do something! It's totally out of control!"

"Six, you idiot! Why'd you do that?! You knocked out three of our teammates with your dumbass grenade!"

A dragon large enough to level a mansion wildly thrashing about on the ground makes for a pretty intimidating sight.

"How was I supposed to know that would happen?! The dragons in the game don't react like this!"

I make excuses to the expendables as I unload rounds from my assault rifle. However—

"The hell? Our shots aren't working! Someone call in some heavier firepower! I don't have enough points to do it!"

Unfortunately, the clean living I've been doing lately means I'm a tad short of Evil Points.

But unlike me, this lot are pretty scummy, so I'm sure they've still got plenty of points…

"""""……"""""

"Hey!"

I can't help but shout at the expendables for not responding to my request, and they reply testily.

"I mean, what else were we supposed to do?! It's lonely at night in the city!"

"We'd go crazy if we didn't call in stuff from Japan using our points!"

"Hard for you, with a harem squad, to know how bad it is for the rest of us!"

So they spent all their Evil Points on porn, huh?

I want to chew them out, but for some reason, I can't bring myself to do it.

It feels like I did something similar a while back…

"U-urmph…I…I can finally see again…"

As I try to fish out the memory I've sealed deep in the recesses of my brain, Rose's voice brings me back to the present.

"Okay, our weapons aren't doing much to it. You guys take care of it with your magical stuff."

"I can't deal with that rampaging thing! It'll crush me if I get too close! Why don't you use your whateverbuzzsaw, Boss?!"

My whateverbuzzsaw is also a melee weapon.

"Tch, that's a hell of a thing to do to us, you bastard…! I didn't expect to have an ally blind me like that!"

"Heine, let's kill him before we hit the dragon. We're in the woods; we just need to tell them the dragon ate him."

As Rose's eyesight returns, Heine and Russell also get worked up.

"Oh? You two losers have never beaten me before. What makes you think you can do it now? I dare you to try me!"

As I taunt them and gesture for them to come at me, their faces start turning red with indignation…

…before suddenly paling as the blood leaves their features.

"B-Boss…behind…"

The cacophony of the dragon's tantrum has died down.

If the three of them have their eyesight back, then it must mean the dragon…

"Retreat!"

"""""Ahhhhhh!"""""

I start running without bothering to look back, feeling the rumble of the dragon's footsteps behind me.

As I dash forward, I pull the pin from a second flash grenade and toss it over my shoulder.

The flash bang explodes with a loud sound, but I don't hear an accompanying screech of agony from the dragon. Evidently, it's already wised up to the danger posed by my grenades.

Dammit, the flash bangs aren't going to do much to slow it down.

I have no choice. I guess I'll have to use my dependable colleagues as a distraction…!

"…Hey! Where the hell did they go?! Did they use me as bait?!"

I don't know if they turned tail or hid using optical camo, but the three Combat Agents are nowhere in sight.

What assholes! Using their own allies as bait! That's why agents of evil corporations can't be trusted!

…It's then that the griffin, healed by Russell's magic, stands up and gazes intently at Heine, its former owner.

"Isaac, you can move again! Good boy, let us on!"

"…"

When Heine runs over to the griffin, it looks toward the dragon before very clearly turning its head away from Heine.

"What's wrong, Isaac? It's me! You can't have forgotten who I am."

Even as Heine shakes the griffin back and forth, it seems to pout with its beak and bleats.

"Miss Heine, Isaac is upset and thinks you abandoned it in the woods!"

"Heine! Apologize! Apologize to Isaac!"

"Isaac, I-I let you go because I was trying to look out for you! I didn't want to let you go! It hurt to do it... But I didn't have any choice. I was going to be enslaved, so you'd have ended up being abused, too...!"

As Heine and the griffin start playing out their little drama, I use a piece of equipment I just ordered from Earth, an enhanced tear gas bomb, on the dragon.

"Graaaaaaaaaaaaaagh!"

Tear gas works on dragons! I need to tell Alice about this!

I turn to the others intent on running as the dragon is suffering from the tear gas—

"C'mon, listen to me, Isaac. I've known you since you were small. I've always thought of you as my little brother... Ow! Why are you pecking at me?!"

"Miss Heine, Isaac is a girl griffin."

"I was wondering why you chose that name... So you just didn't know?"

"Who cares about all of that! Just hurry up!"

The three of them come to their senses and start to panic.

"I'm so sorry, Isaac! When we get back to Hideout City, I'll use the money Alice gave me to buy you the best meats! And I'm never going to let you go again!"

At Heine's desperate persuasion, the griffin spreads its wings and kneels down, signaling to us to get on.

We all hop on the griffin's back, but it seems our combined weight is too much for it, and it starts thrashing about.

"Hey, what the...? Isaac can usually carry five fully armed orcs. What's weighing us down?!"

"It's the Boss! Technically, it's the Boss's armor that's heavy!"

"Rose, let's just kick him off! ...Hey! Let go of my leg!"

I grab Russell's leg, determined to take him down with me if he so much as tries to kick me off, but then I realize that while I could probably survive a fighting retreat through the woods, these three don't have the experience to avoid becoming a tasty snack.

"You lot are going to owe me when we get back to base!"

I jump off the griffin, activate my R-Buzzsaw, and face off against the cautious dragon.

"I'll buy you some time so you weaklings can get out of here! Even if the dragon follows you, Hideout City defenses should be able to handle it at that point!"

Free of my weight, the griffin spreads its wings and looks up at the sky.

"Boss! If you get back safely, I'll share some of my dinner with you!"

Given how fixated Rose is with food, I guess she's trying to be generous.

"Considering how much you've groped me, I'm pretty sure I'll still be ahead in terms of favors."

"You've hiked up my skirt so often, you owe me! So forget about me repaying you!"

As for these two, I'm going to make them pay with their bodies when we get back to the hideout.

Just then, I hear the sound of the griffin kicking off the ground and taking off behind me.

"Compared to giant robots and transforming superheroes, you're just an overgrown flying lizard! You're nothing compared to a Kisaragi agent!"

"Graaaaaaaaaaaawr!"

"Boss!"

5

I mutter to myself as I dash through the endless woods.

"Okay, that thing isn't just a giant lizard! It's not killable! Heroes go down easier than that!"

Dragons are insane. Seriously bonkers.

They're tough as nails, gigantic, and intelligent.

I slashed at it with the R-Buzzsaw, but when I managed to wound it, the creature flew up into the air and attacked me with its fire breath.

That's not a beast you fight mano a mano. It's the sort of thing you take down in a group using heavy anti-aircraft weapons.

"...Shit, I'm lost."

I somehow manage to lose the dragon by running deeper into the woods, but I don't know which way leads to Hideout City.

There's some sort of magnetic field here in these woods, and like the sea of trees near Mount Fuji, it's messing with my compass.

It's starting to get dark out. Am I gonna have to make camp out here?

Calm down, super veteran agent Six. You've done plenty of wilderness survival in the past.

There's nothing to worry about. You've still got some Evil Points. You'll be fine!

...That's what I try to convince myself of as I venture deeper and deeper into this forest thoroughly hostile to human life when I feel someone's eyes upon me.

I reach down and unholster my pistol from my hip.

"...?"

I hear a silent voice from the bushes in front of me, and a familiar masked face appears.

"It's Little Bashin!"

"...?!"

I was so unnerved at being stuck in the woods that I cling to her.

"Thank god you're here! I got totally lost after being chased around by the dragon!"

Little Bashin is at a loss for how to deal with me clinging to her before she settles on gently patting my hair, as though she's reassuring a small child.

Being soothed by a teenage girl in the middle of the woods probably seems really weird from an onlooker's point of view.

"Oh, don't get the wrong idea. It's not like I was scared, and I would've been fine on my own. But, you know, I need to hurry back to the hideout before my underlings get worried about me."

"—! —!"

She nods as though she understands and continues patting my head.

Clearly, she doesn't understand in the slightest.

"Hey, what are you doing here anyway? And why do you have all these cuts and bruises? They treated you back at the hideout, didn't they?"

"—. —!"

Based on what I can gather from her gestures, after having her wounds treated, she became worried about her village and snuck out of the treatment room.

Even if she's from a warrior tribe, I'm not sure if I should let her go back to her village alone. Oh wait, I've got it!

"I need to ask you a favor. Can you lead me back to the hideout? I'll make sure you get a reward."

Little Bashin nods and takes my hand, leading me as though helping a lost child.

My plan is to ask Little Bashin for a favor then get her to the safety of Hideout City, but I guess she's at an age where she wants to act like the guardian.

"...Hey, hey, are you treating me like a kid because I was freaking out a little earlier? You don't need to hold my hand or anything, I'm fine."

"Raaaaaaa!"

"Grawk!"

Little Bashin suddenly throws her hand ax, and a squeal erupts from the bushes.

Diving into the bush, Little Bashin happily returns with a Deadly Hegg, its head bashed in.

"—!"

As Little Bashin raises both arms and lets out call of victory, I hold out my hand to her.

According to Alice, this forest, which is known as the Great Woods, takes up something like sixty percent of the continent.

It's hardly surprising, then, that the local tribes would develop their own, unique cultures in such a large place.

Though they pose a significant threat to us, these woods are as familiar to the Bashin tribe as their own backyard.

What I'm trying to say is…

"Help me, Little Bashin! There's a bipedal rabbit after me! It's creepy as hell!"

"RAAAAAAAAAA!"

We've wandered quite deep into woods, and we're constantly being attacked by monsters.

But thanks to Little Bashin, the large horned rabbit that had been charging after me is soon filleted.

She skillfully butchers the rabbit with her ax. She seems to be in a good mood now. I guess she's happy we've secured dinner.

"Don't get the wrong idea. I could've easily taken care of that mutant bunny on my own. I just let you handle it because it was so creepy. I'm actually pretty strong."

She nods along to my explanation, wrapping the rabbit meat in a leaf, then rinsing off her hands with water from a little bamboo canteen.

Once clean, she holds out one of her small hands to me.

Having grown a bit more used to being led around by the hand by a child, I clasp her palm without hesitation.

"Whoa?! What was that for? Don't yank me forward like that…"

My objection to suddenly being pulled wilts as I see a snake descending onto the spot I had occupied just a moment earlier.

She holds down the snake's body with her foot and casually lops off its head with her ax.

"...Hey, are the Bashins really losing? Just how bad is the enemy you're fighting?"

"...?"

She tilts her head quizzically as she skins the snake, then wraps its meat in a leaf.

The sun has completely set, and I chew on a piece of dried meat that Little Bashin gave me as she leads me through the woods.

Apparently, Little Bashin has good night vision, and she safely guides me through the dark woods.

I don't know what's going to happen to our relationship with the tribe in the future, but even though enhanced Combat Agents have good night vision, it's probably best we avoid fighting them in the dark.

"—!"

"Oh, it's that crazy flower that almost ate me earlier. Don't worry, I'm wise to it now."

Little Bashin pulls me by the hand and points to a pretty flower about the size of a human head.

There's something that looks like a gem embedded in the middle of each flower. When I tried to grab one earlier, the petals snapped shut like a bear trap.

Then I poked the gem with a little stick, and I discovered that the petals were as sharp as knives.

If Little Bashin hadn't stopped me back then, I might have lost my hand to it.

"—! —!"

She's probably trying to praise me for learning from my mistakes.

She stands on her tiptoes and pats my head again. Pretty sure any respect she had for me is gone.

* * *

After walking through the woods for a while, we arrive at a small spring.

Little Bashin uses gestures to tell me that we're going to take a break.

"All right, *this time* leave it to me. I'll show you the power of science."

Little Bashin tilts her head curiously as she gathers twigs to start a fire. It's time for the fruits of civilization to shine.

When Alice, Viper, and I last went exploring in the woods, Viper was able to do just about everything.

But now that Viper isn't here, I can show off the power of modern man by using lighters and rations and reestablish the pecking order…

"—!"

"…What is that, Little Bashin? Why can you instantly light a fire?"

Little Bashin takes out a shiny red rock and hits it with her ax to easily start a flame.

Again?! The inhabitants of this planet have some next-level survival skills.

Little Bashin then starts sharpening some branches into skewers, impaling the rabbit and snake meat before shaking salt on them and putting them on the fire to cook.

She takes out a large, pot-shaped leaf, placing it on the fire and filling it with water from the spring.

The leaf appears to have high flame resistance, and the water inside eventually comes to a boil.

Little Bashin then refills her bamboo canteen with the boiling water before putting some wild grasses she picked on the way into the remaining water.

It's probably the Bashin tribe's equivalent to tea.

As a pleasant aroma rises from the water, she blows on it through her mask to cool the tea before offering the entire container to me…

"Shit, I've become a loser adult forced to rely on a kid. Fine, dammit, I'll drink the tea. I'll drink it, and I'm grateful, but..."

Little Bashin quizzically tilts her head at me. When I accept the tea, she then offers me one of the meat skewers.

First Alice and now Little Bashin. What is it with me being dependent on teenage girls...?

As we're enjoying tea after our meal:

"...Ah, even I know what's going on here. There's several monsters in this bush."

"—!"

Little Bashin stands up with her ax in hand and shelters me behind her back.

Four Deadly Heggs appear from the bush, realizing that they've been spotted.

Four of these things are a threat even to the warriors of the Bashin tribe, and Little Bashin backs away slowly, stopping when she runs into me.

She glances over her shoulder at me, then looks out at the monsters, determined to attack them. I grab her by the wrist to stop her.

"Don't you know what I do for a living, Little Bashin? I'm a trained fighter."

I smile reassuringly to Little Bashin as she looks up at me.

"This is thanks for guiding me this far. I'll help you this time."

As I draw my pistol from my hip, Little Bashin nods repeatedly in my direction.

I run through the forest carrying Little Bashin as we're chased by a horde of Deadly Heggs.

"Sorry, Little Bashin, I thought it was just those four! I could've handled them if there weren't reinforcements!"

As I carry Little Bashin on my shoulder, she reaches over and lightly pats my head to show that she doesn't mind that we've had to flee.

The first group of Deadly Heggs was evidently just a scouting party.

By the time I'd defeated those four, we'd been surrounded by even more of them.

I blinded them with a flash bang before picking up Little Bashin and making a break for it, but—

Despite the fact that my power armor enhances my physical abilities, it's not enough to outrun these dog-shaped monsters.

As the black shadows grow closer, Little Bashin, still dangling from my shoulder, grips her hand ax.

"RAAAAAAA!"

She swings her weapon at a Deadly Hegg's head as it leaps toward my back.

Little Bashin serves as monster repellent while I run toward the light that I see between the trees.

Once I reach that glow, I can expect support from my colleagues.

We eventually stumble out of the woods and look up at the light…

…to find Hideout City burning.

6

As the residents clean up the burnt debris, I take Little Bashin to the infirmary before heading to the conference room to be briefed by Alice with the other main members of the Kisaragi contingent.

"So while you were off on your recon mission, we were attacked by the dragon that had chased after Heine and the others. Rose and Russell were injured drawing the dragon's attention, but luckily, no one was killed."

The injured chimeras are receiving treatment in the infirmary at the moment.

Given how tough they are, the fact that they're in critical condition shows just how much I underestimated the dragons.

The only buildings that caught fire in Hideout City were the wooden warehouses, and there hadn't been any loss of life. That came as a relief, but the residents still look gloomy.

That's understandable.

"Sheesh, it's a shame my underlings are so useless without me! They couldn't even beat a lizard with all these fortifications and equipment!"

Even though there was a large group of Combat Agents in Hideout City, they weren't able to do anything against the dragon's onslaught.

Expendable A, one of the useless idiots who'd used me as a decoy, snaps back at my hectoring.

"S-shut up, asshole! We tried to fight with the heavy weapons! But our projectile weapons didn't work on it for some reason!"

"Say that again? Always with the lame excuses! Just be honest and admit you guys couldn't handle it and that you can't get anything done without MISTER Combat Agent Six."

I defend myself against Expendable A, who protests my taunting. In an unusual little twist, Alice backs him up.

"No, seriously, our heavy weapons didn't work on it, Six. And we've seen that before."

Mook A stops his attack at Alice's words and Snow follows up.

"Yep. It's the same special ability that the Sand King and that giant cat have. It somehow stops all projectile weapons."

Almost all of the giant monsters we've fought have had the same ability.

I see… In that case, there's not much to do against a flying dragon…

"Got it, dumb-dumb? It's not like we weren't doing *anything*! When we found that our attacks were ineffective, we shifted our focus to evacuating the civilians. Jackass."

"And you've got a big mouth for a little boy who got lost in the woods and had to have Little Bashin escort you back to the city. So who's really the useless one here, huh? HUH?"

Two more of the useless expendables taunt me to repay me for my earlier insults.

As I get into a brawl with these two, someone knocks hesitantly on the conference room door.

"Pardon me. I took a look around the city and am pleased to report there wasn't any visible damage. Thankfully, this shouldn't impact our ability to prepare for winter," Viper says as she enters the room, looking visibly relieved as she delivers the news.

She sees us duking it out and quickly tries to intervene.

"U-um...Mr. Six, evil organization or not, fighting with your coworkers isn't good."

"We're not fighting, Vi. I'm just chastising these useless underlings. The only thing they're good for is fighting, so if they can't be useful at that, they'll be no better than children!"

"Oh yeah? Well, next time the dragon comes along, you can deal with it on your own."

"We're not going to help you even if you come sobbing and begging! We were just lucky Miss Viper was here. *You* wouldn't have stood a chance!"

They're lucky that Viper was here? ...Wait, does that mean...?

"Was Vi the one who drove off the dragon?"

"Oh, yes...When we found out that projectiles didn't work, Miss Alice proposed launching the Combat Agents at the dragon with rockets, so I volunteered... Instead of a rocket, I had Heine's griffin carry me up to the dragon, and I jumped onto it before landing a Demon Lord punch," says Viper, lacking any self-preservation instinct as

always. The Combat Agents, whose job it is to fight, look away in uncomfortable silence.

"Aren't you lot embarrassed about sending our new female leader to fight your battles? And that's not even counting the fact that kids like Rose and Russell put their lives on their line, too..."

"We do feel a little bit guilty! But what were we supposed to do? Miss Viper wouldn't take no for an answer, no matter how much we tried to talk her out of it!"

"We'd be the first to charge in against an opponent we can actually handle! We're thinking up ways to deal with dragons now; we'll get them next time!"

Alice speaks up after we watch the losers make their excuses and slink out of the room.

"The letter from the Bashin tribe mentioned a large number of giant monsters that included dragons. So we should operate under the assumption there's more things like that dragon lurking around."

"I see... Thankfully, I do construction for a living. Combat Agents sure have a dangerous job," the construction worker who's supposed to be a knight says, as though it doesn't concern her in the slightest.

"Well, look who's decided to tuck her tail between her legs and hide! I don't think I've ever met a construction worker who's constantly cosplaying as a knight!"

"W-watch your tone! Calling me a cosplayer is going too far! It's true that the creature that attacked us last night was huge, but surely they're not all that size. Besides, dragons fetch good prices. I can't just let you insult me like that. Fine, I'll join the fight next time, too!"

Viper hesitantly raises her hand to stop our argument.

"Um...I don't wish to interrupt, but...a dragon that small isn't going to be worth much money."

Huh?

"Um, Vi...that thing was a *small* dragon? We barely got away from it with our lives."

"Well, um… The dragon from last night is one of the lowest classes of its kind. It's not weak by any stretch of the imagination, but the ones that are truly feared on this world and fetch the highest prices are the greater dragons. It's not uncommon to refer to them as walking natural disasters…"

I decide then and there that I'm going to go do some construction work with Snow for the time being…

I leave the conference room, fully committed to putting in for a transfer when Alice suddenly calls me over.

"Hey, Six, we're going to file a complaint with Hiiragi."

"I'm a construction worker now. You're gonna have to find someone else."

I quickly turn down Alice's nonsensical proposal.

Heading back into the woods after all that? Not a chance in hell.

"The Hiiragis you're scared of are the Hiiragi tribes in the woods controlling the dragons, right? I'm talking about filing a complaint with the Hiiragi who call themselves an Agency of Order."

Oh, right, they're both called Hiiragi, aren't they?

"Remember what that woman Adelie was saying? The surface-dwelling tribes are their followers. They were there to restore the balance when people on the surface obtained too much power."

That's true. If those brutes really are affiliated with the Agency of Order, then the actions by the tribesmen are a violation of our cease-fire.

"But if they're the ones issuing directions to the Hiiragi tribe, wouldn't it be dangerous to just march into their headquarters?"

Alice raises her lips in a conniving little smile at my question.

"Ten's already infiltrated their base to gather information. Depending on how they choose to respond, I'm going to have him do some explosive demolition work at their base."

7

Having come to the land formerly known as the Kingdom of Torace with Alice, I'm throwing a bit of a tantrum in the castle the Hiiragi call their base.

"How dare you ask an evil organization to schedule an appointment! Just bring that dummy Adelie out to talk!"

"The Apostle, Lady Adelheid, is currently dealing with a local visitor! If you're going to keep causing a scene, we'll call the elite soldiers of Hiiragi to remove you!"

"Oh? We kicked your asses last time. You really wanna test Kisaragi a second time? If you're itching for a fight, we won't pull our punches."

Just as I'm about to brawl with the sentries, a voice calls to us from above.

"It's fine. Let those people through. I'll deal with them in Adelheid's stead."

The guy who calls down to us from one of the castle windows is the handsome fella that's Adelie's boss.

I think his name was Fritz or whatever. We're shown into a rather plainly furnished room.

It seems this is Fritz's personal room. I guess they have no intention of playing nice with someone who was their enemy until recently, even with the cease-fire in place.

Can't just let them insult us like this. I should at least complain about their treatment of us…

"Unfortunately, Adelheid is dealing with a messenger from a country called Grunade who's come to file a complaint and is currently using the meeting room. I'm afraid we'll have to speak in this room instead."

"…I see. Well, we're here without notice, so that's acceptable."

Alice makes it sound like we're being magnanimous, but I'm pretty sure the complaints from Grunade are because of our letter.

"I know why you're here. It's about the monsters controlled by the Hiiragi tribe, yes?"

Fritz smiles confidently, lacing his fingers together on top of the table.

"I thought you'd try to play dumb. I'm glad you've owned up to it. Those Hiiragi pets of yours sent a dragon after us. Our cease-fire should still be in effect. We're here to get answers about this little incident."

Fritz's confident smile doesn't waver at Alice's complaint.

I feel like he's got some sort of ace up his sleeve. And just as I'm thinking that…

"It's true that the Hiiragi tribe has interactions with our organization. However, they regard us as servants of the gods because of our advanced technology and culture. I know Adelheid affectionately calls them our followers, but they're very much beneath us… Or rather they're simply cultists who worship us without our permission."

The door behind the coolly smiling Fritz quietly opens.

And entering the room is a stark-naked Combat Agent Ten, towel over one shoulder and optical camo over the other.

Noticing our presence, Ten raises his hand in greeting.

If he's infiltrating this castle, he should be more careful. What's he doing in this VIP room?

"They adopted the name 'Hiiragi tribe' on their own in an attempt to become closer to us… Still, we have taught them our philosophy and principles, and we occasionally provide them with technologies that we no longer have any use for."

None of what Fritz says registers with me.

It seems this information has caught even Alice by surprise, because she's completely frozen next to me.

Based on the fact that he's still damp and there's steam rising from his body, I figure Ten just finished a bath.

I guess he must have walked out of the bathroom, but how the hell did he scrub himself down without Fritz noticing?

I nudge the frozen Alice with my elbow, and her brain reboots as she returns to her senses.

"...Ah, so your reasoning is that the Hiiragi tribe is acting on their own and that you bear...um, no responsibility. Is that how..."

Based on how much difficulty she's having speaking, I guess she hasn't fully finished rebooting.

Get it together, Alice. We can't have the android losing her composure here. If we don't stay cool, Fritz'll figure out there's something going on behind him.

"We're not that irresponsible. But no doubt you also have had problems in your organization with loose cannons acting on their own, yes? As well as affiliated organizations? Let me apologize for the Hiiragi tribe on their behalf for this unfortunate incident. With that said, we'd like to maintain the current arrangement if you are so willing."

Having finished drying off, Ten reaches into what seems to be a fridge behind the smiling Fritz and takes out a drink.

Stop it! Don't gesture to me to ask me if I want one!

"I-I see. We're willing to forgive if you're willing to apologize. Ahm... Then what should we do about those brutes...?"

Alice isn't able to show her usual bravado. Maybe she's not good at dealing with unexpected developments.

Just then, Ten begins communicating with us using hand signs and gestures.

"As noted earlier, they're a group that worships us, rather than a direct subordinate group. You can do whatever you want with them."

<Vital information. Fritz. A Woman. Pretending to be a man.>

...Because Ten tells me this at this vital juncture, I can't process a single word Fritz is saying.

I mean, sure, Fritz looks a bit delicate for a man, and despite the huskiness, his voice is a bit on the high side, but is that really information we need to know right now? Ten's gotta be enjoying this.

"Um, then... You don't mind if we retaliate against them?"

Ignoring Alice's continued confusion, Ten begins communicating again with hand signs.

<Show you. Evidence.>

No. The fact that Fritz is a woman doesn't matter.

My silent plea goes unheard, and Ten casually opens a dresser, digging through it.

"Yes, I have no problem with that. Still..."

Ten then dons the women's underwear he retrieved from the dresser without a moment's hesitation.

<<See?>>

Who the hell cares?! Why did you have to put them on?! Why are you being so disruptive at such an important moment? I bet you're earning Evil Points as we speak, you asshole! We're trying desperately to hold it together right here. Don't go posing to try to make us break character!

"The technology they're using, while obsolete for us, is more than advanced enough to cause you problems. After all, it's even capable of controlling lesser dragons."

I reach my limit and look down at the ground, my shoulders trembling.

Fritz smiles confidently, thinking that my response means that he—or rather, *she*—has the upper hand...

"They're going to be more of a challenge than you think. I wish you the best of luck with your retribution."

Um, you've got a middle-aged man dressed in women's underwear sleeping in your bed.

* * *

On our way back from our meeting with Hiiragi.

Sitting in the passenger seat of the speeding buggy, I turn to Alice in the driver's seat and speak up.

"Why did you pick Ten to infiltrate their base? It's way harder to choke back laughter in the middle of a serious situation like that!"

"Don't make it sound like that was my fault. The problem is with you Combat Agents in general. Just what are you eating that makes you so stupid and impulsive?"

I'm pretty sure that eccentricity is part and parcel of being a Combat Agent. It's a little late to complain about that.

"Anyway, we have their word now. As for the question of taking in the Bashin children, we'll do one better—we'll help the Bashin in their fight. This is a proxy war between an evil corporation and the Agency of Order."

"Meaning, it's a proper combat assignment for the first time in a while. I wish I could say leave the fighting to us, but…"

The problem is that the enemy's controlling giant monsters that are immune to bullets.

We simply don't have the firepower to deal with them.

Even if we drag out the Destroyer, it can't reach a dragon if it's flying.

"I get your concerns. Leave that part to me. We just need to rely on our most powerful asset."

Well, our most powerful asset at the moment is pretty obvious.

Whatever his faults, he takes care of his own, and I'm sure he'll come right on over if he hears Rose and Russell are in the hospital.

Then there's the fact that we're protecting Little Bashin and the other Bashin children.

Given his unfortunate proclivities, I'm sure it'll be easy to motivate him if we get Little Bashin to ask.

Above all else, he's already defeated a dragon after a massive fight and taken its sorcery stone.

It's time for Kisaragi's most powerful mutant, an expert in woodlands combat, currently lurking in the forests of a kingdom called Grunade, to shine.

It's time for Tiger Man, our ultimate mutant, to lay down the law!

[Intermission 1]
—Hello Miss, Nice to Meet You—

I hear a familiar voice address me.

"How are you feeling? No headaches or nausea?"

I crack my eyes open and see a woman in a lab coat peering in on me.

...My head feels a little fuzzy, I tell the woman in front of me.

"That's natural. The medicine I injected is supposed to restore your memories. It's putting strain on your brain, so the fuzziness is normal."

Why did you inject me with that?

"What do you mean why? It's to restore your old personality. I don't think you remember, but after modifying various parts of your body, you need regular maintenance. And at the end of every maintenance session, we always try to restore your memories."

Not having those memories doesn't bother me...

"We can't just leave you like this. It's my fault you've ended up an airhead. No matter how long it takes, I'll get you back to normal."

...Can I ask what you've tried so far?

"...Hypnosis, mostly. I'm pretty confident we'll get somewhere this time. We're combining the hypnosis that had a little bit of an effect last time with a special medicine. I put you into a trance and dig up old memories from the recesses of your mind."

...Did the hypnosis really work last time?

It's hazy, but I remember being made to do something awful last time...

The woman shakes her head, as if she's offended at my hesitation.

"I wasn't just playing around, okay?! I just ordered you to do something you wouldn't normally do, just to make sure you were properly hypnotized! All that involved was having you read some erotica out loud. Don't worry about it."

......

When I fall silent, the woman coughs as though to change the subject.

"So let's get started! Right now, you're back in your distant past. The way you're talking is proof of that! Okay, we'll start with introductions. Tell me your current situation."

Name... My name... And right now, I'm—

"My name is Yukari Sanjo... And tomorrow's the first day of elementary school..."

"That's too far back!"

CHAPTER 2

Belial Arrives...

1

When we arrive at the training ground, we're welcomed by a wide grin.

"Tee-hee, I'm here."

Just what the hell is going on? What is Belial the Great Flame, Kisaragi's single greatest combat asset, doing here?

I turn to Alice and whisper in a voice only she can pick up.

"I thought we were gonna go pick up Tiger Man! Why is Lady Belial here?!"

"The fighting on Earth has settled down a bit, and Lady Belial didn't have anything else to do. Unlike last time, when we had to con Lady Lilith into coming over, the hideout teleporter's stable and working normally, so we were able to borrow Lady Belial under the condition that we send her back the moment we get a recall request from Earth."

Of the three Supreme Leaders, Belial is the only one who has no paperwork to do.

Technically, it's because she *can't* do paperwork. But if we're just having firepower lying idle on Earth, I suppose the logic is that we may as well make use of it here.

It's true that she's probably the one we'd want here more than anyone else, but she's just generally way too quick to act.

"Alice, do you even understand what sort of woman Lady Belial is? In some ways, she's even more problematic than Lady Lilith!"

"I've heard she's unreasonable and prone to solving everything with brute force. That's fine. It's not like Kisaragi's got any normal people in its ranks. I've already accounted for any possible complications."

If Alice has already accounted for all of that, I guess it's fine, but there's something that's been bugging me about Belial.

"Lady Belial, may I ask a question?"

"What is it, Six? Go ahead," says Belial as she puffs out her chest.

"I just have to ask. Why are you dressed like that? What happened to your super-sexy Supreme Leader uniform?"

She had been wearing a uniform that looked like a swimsuit before, but she's now wearing a custom set of red power armor.

"It's because you called it a cheap porn star costume!"

I was just giving my opinion of it, but it seems my remark had bothered Belial, since she was so pure at heart.

"It's fine that you're wearing combat armor, but why are you accentuating your breasts by using belts to give them a boost? Why do you always have to make your clothes look so slutty?!"

"Stop calling your boss slutty! I can't help it, my chest fastener won't stay put," says Belial, even as she naturally exudes raw sex appeal.

"So what's the situation? Who am I supposed to incinerate?"

The sexy Supreme Leader starts out with a scary statement.

"There's this group called the Hiiragi tribe in the woods who control giant monsters. So we need you to take care of them. But first, let me introduce my loyal subordinates."

There's a reason I'm introducing them despite the fact that Belial isn't staying long.

The reason my other colleagues haven't moved a muscle is because they're trying to avoid drawing her attention.

"Hey, Heine, come over here! This is Lady Belial, one of Kisaragi's Supreme Leaders."

Just when I gesture to Heine to come over and introduce herself...

"So you're the copycat from the reports!"

"C-copycat?! What do you mean copycat?!"

Heine, cowed by Belial's sudden anger, takes a step backward.

"You call yourself Heine of the Flames, don't you?! I'm Belial the Great Flame! Your title's too close to mine! Change it!"

"Why?!"

Heine bites her lip and responds to Belial's introductory salvo of reasonable demands.

"R-respectfully, the title is one that was given to me by the Demon Lord as the strongest fire magic user in the army. It means a lot to me. Even if it's close to yours, I can't just go and change it..."

Oh right, Heine always seems happy when she's referred to as one of the Elite Four or Heine of the Flames.

...But.

"I don't care about any of that! From this day forward, you're just plain Heine! Also, your voice sounds way too much like mine, and you talk too much like me! Shift your voice up half an octave and stop pronouncing your *r*'s!"

"That's not fair at all!"

If I were to add a comment of my own, they're also similar in that they've got flaming hot bodies.

Heine protests, but logic has no sway against Belial, a force of nature against whom reason means little to nothing.

In terms of combat, there's no one I'd rather have on my side than Belial, but outside of the battlefield, there's all sorts of things wrong with her.

The reason I introduced Heine to her was to try and have her share the burden that is this belligerent and unreasonable woman.

"All right, then, Heine! Since you're both fire users, you're going to be Lady Belial's guide here. Make sure you treat her with respect!"

I was also hoping to dump Belial off on Heine, who I assumed would be something of a kindred spirit.

"No. It's been too long since I've seen you, Six. I want you to be my guide."

2

Heine murmurs blankly at the sight in front of her...

"Lady Belial certainly moves quickly..."

Belial's only been on the planet for about an hour, but our brutal boss has already begun setting fire to this planet's forests as part of her introductory tour.

She said she wanted to see the hostile life-forms, so we've brought her to the Great Woods.

After Belial demanded that I be her guide, Heine and I accompanied her to the forest. As we stand at a distance watching her unleash her hellfire at the woods, silhouettes begin moving among the flames.

"Oh hey, Six, some weird women showed up."

"Those ladies come out when you set the forest on fire. They're like guardians of some sort. They split their heads and fire cannonballs out of them, so please be careful!"

Belial was granted pyrokinesis by undergoing Lilith's mad scientist brain surgery.

Her firepower is so overwhelming that she's on par with a small arsenal; she's basically dropped any and all pretenses of being human.

"Have you forgotten who you're talking to, Six?! Bullets aren't going to do much to me!"

"...Well, yes, but it doesn't hurt to be safe."

The enhancement surgery also cranked up Belial's defenses and physical abilities to superhuman levels, so she prefers leading from the front.

"Ah! It...doesn't hurt? It doesn't hurt at all! Stop looking at me like that, Six! I said it doesn't hurt!"

"I get it, so please hide. There's no reason to go out of your way to get hit by them."

"How is she still alive after taking a round from the forest guardians...?"

Ignoring Heine's naked awe at Belial's toughness, the stubborn Supreme Leader holds back tears from the enemy attacks and swiftly hides behind the tree line.

At the same time, the burning trees begin spraying water from their branches to start dousing the flames.

"Hey, do they have sprinklers embedded in them?!"

"This planet's forest puts out its own fires. Because of that, we haven't been able to do any slash-and-burn agriculture."

Belial nods, impressed by this discovery, and retrieves something from her pocket.

"So what you're saying is that we need more firepower to burn down these woods."

"Um, I don't think that's it at all, but if that's what makes sense to you, Lady Belial, sure."

Nodding to herself, Belial injects the ampule into her neck.

The cartridge is mostly made up of nitro. It's a booster that enhances Belial's pyrokinesis.

If she overuses it, she's pretty much useless the next day, but since she seems to have no ability to learn from her own mistakes, she never hesitates to use the injections no matter how much we try to stop her.

The nitro flows into Belial's veins, and her eyes become bloodshot and shimmer.

"Hey, rookie! Make sure you take notes! So long as we have enough firepower, we flame wielders are unmatched!"

"Y-yes, ma'am!"

Belial smirks happily at Heine's respectful response and sticks out her hand from behind the tree.

"Taaaaaake thaaaaaaaaaaaaaat!"

As Belial's shout rings out, a huge inferno erupts from the middle of the forest—!

"I see, so that's the cause of all this."

The shockwave from Belial incinerating a chunk of the forest as a little introduction to this world wiped out all the glass windows in Hideout City.

The sudden explosion sent the residents of the city into a panic, and the Grace Kingdom had sent a messenger to check in.

After cleaning up our mess, Alice makes us sit contritely in a corner of the glass shard–infested conference room.

"Sorry, Alice. I did my usual attack without considering where I was. I mean, all of the windows in our base on Earth have reinforced glass, right? And besides, the people over there are used to explosions."

Belial looks apologetic, scratching the back of her head as she musters an apology.

"No, it's not your fault, Lady Belial. I called you here with the understanding there'd be the occasional problem. It's these two who are at fault for not properly backing you up."

"Hold on a minute! I can't be at fault here! I had no idea just how powerful Lady Belial was!"

Heine had changed her tone of voice and accent after witnessing Belial's firepower.

"Oh? You trying to pin all the blame on me, then? Well, that's a compliment for a Kisaragi employee! You're also one of Lady Belial's companions! You can't be the only one who dodges responsibility!"

"You've known Lady Belial a long time, right, Six?! Then you should've been able to see this coming!"

Alice lets out an exasperated sigh as we start bickering.

"All the windows here at the hideout are goners, but considering Lady Belial's accomplishments, it's a small price to pay. After all, she opened up a huge clearing in the woods that we've been trying to develop. Once we fill in the crater, we can start building immediately."

I'm told Belial's maximum firepower is the equivalent of ten thousand tons of TNT.

I don't know how powerful that actually is, but one of Belial's strengths is that she can shoot off blasts like that with ease by using just a single nitro cartridge.

"Besides, even I didn't expect Lady Belial to start her campaign as soon as she arrived. But now that Kisaragi's ultimate weapon is here, the Hiiragi tribe doesn't stand a chance.

Alice, who is a fervent believer in the power of Kisaragi science, holds up her fist triumphantly.

"We can't let them think they can attack an evil corporation and get away with it! We'll gather our Combat Agents tomorrow and go save the Bashin tribe's village!"

"Yeah! It's time to avenge our chimeras! We'll make the enemy suffer for what they've done!"

As Alice and Heine work themselves into a lather, Belial leans over and whispers:

"Hey, why can't we just go now...?"

I wish Belial could give even a tenth of her motivation and initiative to that lazy brat Lilith.

* * *

The next day.

"Urgh… Six, gross…"

"Why are you calling me gross this early in the morning?"

Belial insults me the moment I arrive to pick her up from her room.

"Not what I meant… I feel gross… My head hurts…"

"That's because you used a nitro cartridge yesterday. This is why I keep telling you to stop using those; they're so bad for you."

Belial's robe is only loosely draped around her body, and she's pale, as though she's badly hungover. She reaches over and grabs a nitro cartridge.

"Best thing to do when I feel like this is to take a shot in the morning."

"You sound like a drunkard talking about the hair of the dog. I'm not letting you use a cartridge just so you can ease your withdrawal."

Belial glares at me as I snatch the cartridge away.

"Give me back my precious…"

"I can't. Lady Lilith warned me not to let you use too many."

As I gently push the wobbly Belial back into her room so she can change, I hear something heavy fall to the ground behind me.

I turn to find the source of the noise…

"Commander… What's the precious thing you took from this skanky woman?"

Grimm stands there staring at me.

There's a picnic basket, probably filled with sandwiches or something, lying on the floor at her feet.

"What did you take from that hungover and super skanky-looking woman? Her robes are undone… What's the precious thing you took?!"

"It's too early for your histrionics. I took this from her, okay? One of Lady Belial's nitro cartridges."

Grimm's expression rapidly returns to normal as I show her the cartridge.

"...Lady Belial? The name's familiar..."

"She's one of Kisaragi's Supreme Leaders. She's my boss and one of the most important people in the company."

Grimm sits down formally, bowing deeply to Belial.

"Our Commander's in your debt, Lady Belial. I am his subordinate and fiancée, Grimm Grimoire. We may be inexperienced, but we hope that you will continue to provide us with your guidance."

"Stop telling everyone you see that we're engaged. You're going to end up regretting it."

I can't help but interject, prompting a wide-eyed stare from Grimm.

"What do you mean I'll regret it?! You can't get out of it now!"

"I'm just trying to tell you that if you go around telling people you're engaged, there won't be any guys coming your way."

I pick up the basket and hand it over to Grimm as she seems lost in contemplation. Belial, who seems to have recovered from her nausea, turns to us and speaks.

"I see your weird charms are still working. What's with this fiancée stuff?"

"I just promised I'd marry her if we were both single in ten years. Though, I have every intention of getting married to someone else before that."

"What a terrible thing to say in front of your fiancée."

Belial gazes intently at Grimm, who hugs the basket and mutters to herself.

"Hey, Grimm, was it? Why are you barefoot?"

"It's a religious thing. If I wear shoes or socks, terrible things happen," Grimm says with a smile, answering a common question thrown her way upon making a new acquaintance.

"...Six, let's put some socks on her."

"We can't, Lady Belial. If I'm right, that'll just kill her."

But Belial's eyes are shimmering with curiosity.

"That's ridiculous, no one dies because they put on socks. And besides, I'm a Supreme Leader in an evil organization. Telling me that someone doesn't want to do something makes me want to do it even more."

"No, no, this one dies all the time. The moment I let her out of my sight, she always gets killed by the most idiotic and useless thing."

Even as I say this, Belial takes out her portable teleporter and a memo pad.

Seems she's serious about this. If I don't do something, Grimm's going to croak.

"...Hey, Commander, she's not serious, is she? I brought you breakfast because I wanted to feed you. I'm a great catch, aren't I? Whyever would you want to let such a wonderful fiancée die in your presence?"

"Listen, Grimm, when I give the signal, run as fast as you can. Belial's the sort who doesn't listen once she gets an idea into her head. I'll throw myself in front of her to distract her. If you avoid her long enough, she'll forget what she was trying to do."

As though sensing the seriousness of my tone, Grimm pales as she slowly backs away.

However, instead of running, she softly sets the basket she's been hugging to her chest onto the floor.

"Commander, I put more work into today's sandwiches than usual. I'm pretty confident in them. They use high-grade Chirping Mole meat. When this battle's finished, let's have them together in the courtyard."

"Don't use meat I've never heard of. I'll decide whether to eat it or not after seeing what the original animal looks like... But that's completely beside the point. You need to run! We couldn't even beat her with a small army!"

Grimm lightly presses her index finger to her lips and smiles sweetly.

"I'm not just a pretty face to be protected, you know. I'm not the type of rational, calculating woman who can abandon her fiancé when he's about to put his life on the line for the girl he loves. Heh, if I could do that, I would've married some rich and handsome man a long time ago…"

"I'm not trying to put my life on the line. Also, calling yourself the girl I love is a bit of an exaggeration."

Grimm ignores my comment and produces a large number of rings from her pocket.

"These are all the fruits of love that I gathered from patrolling the nighttime streets! The affection of these men and women will now—"

"Hraagh!"

Grimm is so caught up in the moment that she has no time to react as Belial cuts right through her speech and tackles her from below.

Damn, no wonder she's considered Kisaragi's best. Even I could barely react.

"Welp, it's too late now that Lady Belial's caught you. Oh well, I'll go gather some offerings to put on the altar."

"Don't give up so quickly! I thought you were going to protect me, Commander!" Grimm wails as Belial pins her to the ground. Alas, the most I can do when facing a Supreme Leader is buy some time…

"That's why I told you to run, dammit… Excuse me, Lady Belial, she's still one of my subordinates. I can't have her dying…"

"Here we go!"

It's not that Belial can't read the room, it's that she doesn't want to bother doing so. And after completely ignoring Grimm's and my exchange, she forces a pair of socks onto Grimm's feet.

3

After placing Grimm's body on the altar, we make our way to the gathering point where we find three expendable Combat Agents, Heine, and our guide, Little Bashin.

The girl looks happy that we're going to save her village, holding her ax over her head in a cheerful gesture.

"What now, Lady Belial? Grimm isn't going to revive for a while."

"I have no idea what you're talking about with this revival stuff. Remember? The enhancement surgery wiped out part of my memory."

Why would surgery that happened years ago wipe out her short-term memory, exactly? Oh well, I guess she's just trying to pretend that the little dustup with Grimm never happened.

Having set those recent unpleasant memories aside, Belial turns to the group and raises her voice.

"All right, we're all here! Agents, roll call!"

"Six!"

"Fifteen!"

"Seventeen!"

"Twenty-nine!"

"...!"

"Um...what am I supposed to...?"

After we each yell out our own numbers, Belial comes and gives each of us a light smack.

"I didn't tell you to call out your names! Whatever! So four agents and two locals, right? So counting me, that's seven total. All right, the mission continues even if we suffer light wounds, but we'll scrap it if we lose someone."

"You could at least say something motivational, like, 'We'll finish this without losing anyone!' We do have feelings, Lady Belial."

Sigh. Lilith, Alice, they're all the same, treating us Combat Agents like we're expendable. That's why Kisaragi has a reputation for ruthlessness.

Belial blinks as she looks over in our direction.

"Don't be stupid. You've got me on your side, so there's no way any of you are going to die. I'll make sure to protect you all. If we're gonna lose anyone at all, I'll make sure it's me."

"You know, you should really warn us before you say something like that. You made my heart skip a beat."

Yeah, despite the fact that she can be unreasonable and overbearing, sometimes she can cut through your defenses and hit you right in the feels.

As my colleagues look down a little shyly, Heine, whose cheeks are faintly flushed, whispers to me.

"Hey, Six, is it just me or is Lady Belial one of the good bosses?"

I don't know if she's one of the good ones or not, but I do know that she's simply a good person at heart.

It's been several hours since Little Bashin started leading us through the woods.

From deep in the brush, we hear drumming of some sort—signals, it seems—from the Bashin tribe.

"...!"

When she hears them, Little Bashin glances up sharply and begins to gesture rapidly. It seems she's trying to tell us something, but we can't tell what she's trying to say.

Given the fact that she's blocking the direction the sound is coming from and crossing her arms in a big X, is she trying to tell us not to go that way?

"If you have something to tell us, speak up!"

"...?!"

Our unreasonable boss has no qualms about yelling at the tribal child.

It's not that she can't talk, it's just that her grasp of the common tongue isn't the strongest.

Little Bashin shakes her head intently to try to communicate this to Belial, but...

"Try telling me what's going on in front of us. I get that you're so shy, you have to wear a mask, but now's not the time to be bashful, is it?"

Um, pretty sure she doesn't wear a mask just because she's shy.

Little Bashin spends a few moments lost in thought before pressing her mask to Belial's ear.

"—. —!"

"See? You can talk when you need to."

Belial approvingly pats Little Bashin on the head.

"To explain… 'The village ahead is under attack by a large group of giant monsters and dragons, and the situation is grim. The adults have set fire to the village in the hopes of taking the monsters down with them, while the children are to find shelter with Kisaragi.'"

Belial continues to speak coolly, not even bothering to face us.

"And this little one's saying, 'We can't involve you further in our fight; let's turn back.'"

She then glances down at Little Bashin, who accepts the patting without complaint.

"You all know what we need to do. Don't let me down, dammit."

When Little Bashin turns her head up to look at Belial in the face, the Supreme Leader smiles reassuringly and, without a second's thought about the side effects, injects herself with a nitro cartridge.

"Let's go, you apes! Chaaarge!"

""""""Yahooo!""""""

"RAAAAAAAAAAAAA!"

"W-wait, don't leave me!"

Her eyes bloodshot from the nitro cartridge, Belial charges forward with a band of bloodthirsty Combat Agents in tow—

"Lady Belial leapt in and incinerated the forest and the monsters."

"Why can't you write a better report?"

Alice presses for details as I write up my report.

"Eleven twenty, arrived at the Bashin village under attack. Eleven twenty-one hours, Lady Belial unleashed a jump kick on the lesser dragon leading the monsters, defeating it instantly. Afterwards, Lady Belial incinerated the dragons and monsters who were attacking the village along with the village itself."

"Why would you let her do that?"

Don't ask me.

"I didn't even have time to try to stop her. The moment we ran into the enemy, a dragon—you know, a creature that's supposed to be *immune* to fire—gets blasted away by a kick and bursts into flames. I think we just need to feel lucky that there weren't any casualties."

Alice crosses her arms in thought as she digests my explanation.

"...And? Where is Lady Belial herself?" Alice asks as she notices Belial herself is absent.

"Well, she felt bad for accidentally burning down the Bashin village, but she said she could balance the scales by burning down the other one, too. Then she ran off in the direction of the Hiiragi village."

"Go get her. NOW," Alice says with a serious expression.

"To be honest, I don't think we'll make it in time. Apparently, the Hiiragi village isn't too far from the Bashin village."

Right on cue, the plastic sheeting covering the broken windows flutters as a giant pillar of fire erupts from the forest.

"...I was hoping we could get the technology or whatever they were using to control the monsters."

"I'm pretty sure it's gone up in smoke by now."

Still, this means the enemy tribe is gone, making our invasion all that much easier.

"Six, what was the point of Fritz from the Hiiragi Agency of Order looking so confident when they told us that the Hiiragi tribe was tougher than they looked and that they wished us luck in our retribution? I mean, the dragon was wiped out pretty much instantly, and the Hiiragi tribe went down almost as an afterthought."

"Either way, everything worked out in the end. Although the

Bashin village burned down, the adults who were planning to go out in a blaze of glory wound up surviving. When Lady Belial gets back, we should thank her with a feast."

There's actually a reason I've come back on my own.

Belial said that she wanted to eat some local delicacies when she got back to the hideout.

I don't know why that thought occurred to her just then, but I figured I'd get back early and surprise her with a roast orc's head.

"...Yeah, true. The moment a Kisaragi Supreme Leader showed up, I knew peace wouldn't be an option. Given that the problem was taken care of so quickly, I guess it's better than when Lady Lilith was here. Since it was quite an ask to get HQ to send us Lady Belial in the first place, I'm just glad we can send her back after only two days. Let's try to at least make her feel appreciated tonight and send her back to Earth in a good mood."

"Lady Belial's pretty easy to please. Just point her in the direction of a powerful enemy. However..."

As I'm about to finish my sentence, one of my colleagues reports in via radio.

"This is Combat Agent Fifteen. Burning the village went according to plan, but Lady Belial started chasing the fleeing monsters and Hiiragi tribesmen. We're going to lose sight of her..."

"...When she finds an enemy, she charges in without thinking, ends up getting separated from the others, and usually gets lost."

"After her!" shouts Alice, in a rare moment of panic.

4

As the sun sets, several of my colleagues return with Hiiragi tribesmen prisoners in tow.

Since Belial is nowhere in sight, it's safe to assume that no one was able to keep up with her.

"...This is a problem. They let us borrow Lady Belial from HQ on the condition we send her back the moment they need her. I won't have any way of making it up to them if something happens to her."

Alice, having barged into my room, flops onto my bed, pattering her feet like the child she appears to be. She lets out a soft sigh.

We've sent out search parties, but so far, we haven't heard anything from them.

It'd be easier to track Belial if she'd just request food and water from Earth, but unfortunately, she's got quite a bit of survivalist training, too, so she's able to function for a long time without fueling up.

Although, with all that said, Belial's from a rich family. Maybe she'll want to avoid having to camp out and order a prefab cottage and supplies to be teleported to her once it gets dark.

"Lady Belial will eventually just come back without a care in the world. It's all because this planet's a backwater without cellphone service. Let's have Lady Lilith create a smartphone that can be used without cell towers."

"...Well, I suppose Kisaragi's most powerful leader isn't going to struggle against any mere monsters. We'll continue with the search parties, but let's hope Lady Belial contacts us herself. If HQ asks for her, we'll just have to find some way to hold them off."

As though timing it perfectly with the end of Alice's grousing...

A desperate scream echoes from our rarely used underground dungeon...

"Hiss! Hiss!"

In the dimly lit dungeon, a fired-up Little Bashin bangs on the bars with her hand ax.

The target of her intense hostility is a woman cowering at the far end of the cell.

"You can't do that, Little Bashin. She's a valuable prisoner. We want their technology, so we can't have you going around executing them willy-nilly."

Little Bashin, who's been trying to break down the bars to the cell with her ax, looks up at me when I intervene and slumps her shoulders.

Even though the scene should make me think there's a crazed ax murderer trying to assault a poor woman in a dimly lit dungeon, I can't help but feel a pang of sympathy for the girl.

Alice turns to Little Bashin and offers reassuringly:

"I know you want to get revenge on your longtime enemy, which I'm happy to let you have, but it'll have to wait until I'm done with the interrogation."

"Wait, don't be offering up lives like that! Isn't this woman the head of the Hiiragi tribe?"

When Belial assaulted the village, most of the Hiiragi tribesmen escaped, but our forces managed to capture a handful of them.

So the plan became that we needed to have some answers about all the mysteries that surrounded these weird tribesfolk, and it progressed into interrogations, but...

"Our long-term objective is to move all of humanity from Earth to this planet. While there's plenty of undeveloped land at the moment, this place will eventually be full of people from Earth. It wouldn't be such a bad idea to cull the herd a little beforehand..."

"C'mon, that's way too heartless, even for an android! ...Hold on a second. I thought I was sent to this planet to look for work opportunities for Combat Agents for when Kisaragi finished conquering Earth. Do we really need to bring everyone over from Earth?"

To my question, Alice responds with a simple smile.

"Well, yeah, we can't let you Combat Agents get thrown out into the street with nowhere to go. Kisaragi's a corporation that prides itself on taking care of its own."

......

"Wait, what's going on with Earth anyway? Is there something wrong with it? The heroes blowing up my apartment isn't the only reason my requests for leave keep getting denied, is it?!"

"Come on, it's time to get down to interrogating. Rejoice, Six—the chieftain is a woman. You love this sort of thing, don't you?"

"Well, yeah, I don't mind it, but answer my questions, dammit!"

Just then:

"The minds of savages are filled with such base thoughts."

The Hiiragi chief locked up in the cell murmurs almost to herself.

Having been stripped of her mask when she was taken prisoner, the woman looks over at us with defiant eyes. They have a faintly feline insolence and ferocity to them, and her gaze makes it all too clear that she views us as inferior.

I'm told the chief fought as part of the rearguard during Belial's assault, buying time for the rest of her people to escape.

"Are you calling *us* savages? Hmph. Well, never mind that. I didn't realize you could speak properly. I was planning to make Viper interpret, but this saves a lot of time."

"The Hiiragi tribe is far superior to you all. As such, we are capable of speaking your simple, barbarian tongue."

Yes, we can understand her, but she kind of sounds like she's going through one of those translation websites or something.

"...By the way, the member of the Bashin tribe over there also speaks your barbarian tongue on a daily basis. The markings on her body aren't even permanent and can be removed by rubbing on them. She's simply *pretending* to be of a primitive tribal culture."

"?!"

Little Bashin shakes her head furiously, rejecting the chief's words.

"—! —!!"

"Okay, I get it, it's fine. You don't need to let us wipe at your tattoos to prove they're real. I believe you!"

I try to calm Little Bashin as she pushes a cloth toward me, as though trying to get me to attempt to wipe the tattoos away. As she watches our exchange, the chief suddenly breaks out laughing.

"Heh-heh-heh! A jest! I'm only kidding. The Bashin tribe are known for being quite serious. Bah-ha-ha-ha!"

"Hsss! Hrrr…!"

Little Bashin resumes bashing on the bars with her ax, prompting the chief to back up just a smidgen before she waves her hands tauntingly at the girl.

"It will take a great deal of time to break the bars with that ax! Keep going! Keep going! Bah-ha-ha-ha-ha! This taunting is retribution for your continued resistance and interference in our activities! And it appears to have caused the Bashin individual quite a bit of distress!"

"RAAAAAAAAAAAAAAAA!"

As Little Bashin angrily smacks the bars with her ax, Alice quietly hands her the key.

"We've got a few more prisoners we can question. So you can do what you want to this one."

"Hrrrrmph! Hiss!"

"Bashin girl, cool your head! My apologies for the taunts! However, our peoples have long been hostile to one another! Try to understand *our* feelings on the matter!"

The chief sobs apologetically to Little Bashin as she takes the key and tries to unlock the cell.

"…Listen up. I'm sure you've realized this by now, but unless you give serious answers to my questions, I'm going to sic her on you, got it?"

"Understood."

The chief's face twitches nervously as Little Bashin waves the key to underline the fact that she's the one in control.

"Then why don't we get the fun started? Heh-heh, Lady Chieftain, you do understand what happens to women who get captured by an evil organization, don't you?"

"Come to think of it, we do owe them payback for attacking us with solar rays and interfering with our construction. Let's get her to fess up about how they managed that little bit of terrorism."

The chief pales as Alice and I let out malicious chuckles, prompting an eager round of applause from Little Bashin.

Given that they commonly bash people's heads in, the Bashins appear to have no real aversion to this sort of violence.

"I'm Alice Kisaragi, the de facto leader of this joint, and this is Combat Agent Six."

"A pleasure to meet you. I am the chief of the Hiiragi clan, Miyabi Hiiragi Archylicia..."

As the chief introduces herself, I whisper into Alice's ear:

"Alice, her name's way too long. There's no way I can remember that."

"You're right. It's a hassle to even bother learning it. From here on out, you're just Savage A."

"...I am now Savage A. I acknowledge this designation. Alice Kisaragi, what do you wish to learn from Savage A?"

There's a bunch of things we'd like to know, but...

Savage A sits on the ground, holding on to the bars of the cell as she looks quizzically at Alice, prompting the android to squat down and stare directly at the captive.

"First things first, tell me about the solar ray attacks. Given that there aren't any satellites in orbit, where are you firing those things from?"

"We send the coordinates to the floating fortress in the sky and request support fire from them."

...Floating fortress.

"Oh, that's right. When we were parachuting down from the upper atmosphere, there was no sign of that castle, yet the thing appeared out of nowhere while we weren't looking. Where the hell did that thing sprout from?"

"The castle did not sprout; it was always there. That fortress is the main headquarters of the Hiiragi Agency of Order. It's usually protected by an optical shield keeping it hidden from savage eyes. That is why you were unable to see it."

Alice and I exchange glances at Savage A's words.

"<Hey, Alice, she just said something about an optical shield. They seriously have technology that's on par with ours, don't they?>"

"<The fact that she understands what a solar ray is must be proof that something is off. Some elements of their technology are actually ahead of Earth's.>"

As we exchange whispers in Japanese, Savage A just chuckles confidently.

"The Hiiragi Agency of Order is truly remarkable. I have no doubts that their might will overwhelm you. That being said, things will go more smoothly for you if you treat a Hiiragi affiliate like myself with respect."

Seems like our exchange has given her the confidence to take the conversational offensive.

"Hey, there was another thing I wanted to ask. That officer, Adelie. She has a giant cat as a pet, right? Does that mean you guys are the ones who created the Sand King and the Forest King?"

"That is correct. The Hiiragi Agency of Order created the Sand King. But you are also incorrect. The lizard-type mechanical life-form guardian was created by a faction hostile to the Hiiragi Agency of Order. Most of the organic monsters were created by Hiiragi, while the mechanical monsters were created by the enemy."

Savage A is evidently enjoying showing off Hiiragi's technology and continues to lecture us with a confident smirk on the differences between the monsters.

"Hey, this is getting even more complicated. So the giant monsters that are living creatures are Hiiragi products, and the mechanical ones are made by an enemy faction? But where's the enemy group lurking around?"

"Remember that underground facility that the lizard robot known as the Forest King was protecting? I'm betting that was the enemy faction's base or research facility..."

Little Bashin, unable to follow our conversation, begins theatrically sharpening her hand ax.

"Soon you will be met with divine judgment. That is because Hiiragi has embedded a royal family with an anti–Demon Lord gene marker. Indeed, the so-called Chosen One gene will soon become active and wipe out the Demon Lord and the demons. Once that is complete, the next target will be—"

"The Chosen One's missing in action and the Demon Lord's switched employers."

"?!"

...The only sound in the dungeon is the steady scraping of Little Bashin's ax against her grindstone. Alice then continues as though nothing happened.

"When you all kept attacking our Hideout City every time we completed it, what were you trying to accomplish? Do you have a claim to the forest or something?"

"Our role is to destroy buildings created by savages that have forgotten their station and gotten too uppity. The destruction of such buildings is a signal to the Hiiragi Agency of Order to come down from their floating fortress and begin managing the affairs of the savages."

It seems this subject triggered something in Savage A, and she stands up, raises her arms and begins to preach.

"Once, humanity prospered upon this world. They used advanced technology to sustain advanced ways of living, and all enjoyed the fruits of civilization. But humanity outgrew its environment! It was then beset by all sorts of problems: food, living space, declining marriage rates…"

"Don't turn this into some sermon. Keep it as short and simple as you can. Look at them. They're so bored, they've just started doing their own thing."

I sit down next to Little Bashin and begin working on my knife. Savage A gazes over at us longingly, as though she wishes we'd listen.

"…A long time ago there was amazing technology that made the population grow. That caused problems like food shortages, global warming, lack of land, environmental pollution, and all of those problems combined resulted in a war. As a result, some really awful weapons were used, making most of the land uninhabitable."

…Huh.

"<Hey, Alice. Doesn't this planet's past sound a bit like Earth's present?>"

"<Yeah, Earth's got some serious problems because of overpopulation. Even if Kisaragi hadn't started its conquest, the countries of the world would've ended up at each other's throats soon enough anyway. Guess civilizations pretty much burn out the same way, no matter what world they're on.>"

That's depressing. This is supposed to be a strange new world, and instead we're getting the distressing realities of our old world in a different form.

"The enemy faction created genetically modified seeds to restore the wasted land. They're the ones who planted the great woods, and the guardians who protected it. Then they went underground to wait."

"…? I mean, restoring the land is good and all. But the woods have taken over most of the planet at this point, no? That'd be fine if it was just a normal forest, but as far as we can tell, it's an incredibly hostile environment."

"It was a mistake. They went too far with their genetic engineering efforts and were unable to stop the spread of the woods."

Hey.

"Hiiragi created the Sand King in their own effort to restore the lands and to stop the spread of the forests before retreating to the skies.

"…? The Sand King was created to restore the land? That thing was doing the opposite! It was turning perfectly good land into desert."

Well, I mean, sure, it was facing off against the Forest King, I guess.

"Another mistake. The research division heard that moles helped make land more fertile and arable and just decided that if normal moles could do that, then a giant one would do an even better job."

"You and this 'enemy' have several screws loose. This is the sort of stuff evil organizations are supposed to do."

Alice turns to quiz Savage A, as she seems unfazed by my criticism.

"All right, we get your history. But what's the deal with destroying anything 'beyond the civilization's station'? Adelie was insistent that they were on the side of justice and righteousness."

"The great people of Hiiragi once said that the wars and pollution were a product of savages obtaining technology that was beyond their ability to use responsibly. Thus, the great people of Hiiragi came to the conclusion that it was best to leave savages as primitive as possible."

"Hey, Alice, these bastards are evil! They're obscurantist elites!"

Put simply, obscurantism is the act of restricting the available knowledge to the people, steadily eroding their level of education to ensure that the masses are too ignorant to question the political status quo. It's such a dangerous piece of governing policy that Kisaragi rejected it after a series of heated debates on the subject.

Evidently offended at being called evil, Savage A grabs the bars and shouts insults in our direction.

"You savages reproduce like rats if left to your own devices! Then you consume all the resources! The ignorant masses need to be managed by the elites in order to prevent the world from being destroyed!"

"Shut up, you moron! If I ever get married, I'll breed every day of the week! You think it's your business to manage people like that?! I'll singlehandedly solve the crisis of declining birth rates!"

"You savages are as crude and uncouth as expected! Idiots like you will be the first to be purged once Hiiragi takes over the world!"

This bitch…

"Try it, I dare you! You don't seem to understand your predicament. Evil organizations have no reservations about putting prisoners in compromising situations!"

"Actually, we do have rules against that."

I give Alice the side-eye at her comment, then unlock the cell door and enter.

Savage A's imagination does the hard part for me, and she starts backing away, holding her hands in front of herself to ward me off.

"I take back what I said earlier… You're a very handsome savage. I will now grace you with a dance of apology."

"What the hell is a dance of apology? Are you messing with me?! Heh-heh, it's too late to grovel. Now, what shall I do with you?"

I let out a creepy little chuckle and approach slowly, when Alice interjects.

"Hold it, Six. I want to see this dance of apology. It actually reminds of the whole 'dancing before the solar ray fires' thing. Why do you do that? Are you using the dance to communicate the attack coordinates?"

Oh, that's right. The Hiiragi tribe did always dance before an attack.

Maybe Alice is right, and the dance is a means of communicating a target to the fortress…

"That dance is a dance of victory and taunting, to tell the target that they are about to be destroyed."

"RAAAAAAAAAAA!"

Little Bashin, who had somehow snuck into the cell, pounces upon Savage A after hearing her ridiculous response.

5

It's been two days since Belial went missing.

The Bashins who lost their village to the fire have started forcing their Hiiragi captives to build a new settlement near Hideout City.

Savage A, who was at serious risk of having her head bashed in, gave a groveling dance of apology to Little Bashin, and is now working for her as an underling.

I see Savage A hauling around construction materials under the watchful eye and hand ax of Little Bashin, but so far, there aren't any problems of note.

Since these two tribes seem to have a long, complicated history, it's probably better to just let them handle it.

The problem that's left for us to solve is to figure out how to find Belial and get her to come home.

As Alice and I chew over this problem, a messenger arrives from a country called Grand Doble.

I've never heard of the place, so I'm caught a bit flat-footed even as I head to the conference room to hear what the messenger has to say.

The messenger from Grand Doble bows his head the moment he enters the room.

"Our country has no intention of making an enemy of Kisaragi. We are prepared to begin diplomatic relations with your company. Ours is a nation rich in high-quality ores, and we can provide them to you at extremely low cost."

"...I see. Our main exports are water crystals and manufactured goods. We don't need you to sell us your ores at too low a cost. So long as it's a little cheaper than the market rate, we're happy to trade."

Despite the fact that this is our first meeting, the messenger is almost excessively respectful. Alice, unfazed by this attitude, deals with him calmly.

The fact that she doesn't ask for details before launching into terms is very in character for Alice, but the small concessions she's making tip me off that she's aware something happened to Grand Doble to make them approach us so meekly.

Even I can see what's driving this. It's gotta be Belial-related.

"T-truly?! Thank you, thank you so very much! I've brought some rare and valuable ores as a gift, so please accept them as a sign of friendship! His Majesty has been extremely anxious about the outcome of our negotiations, so I will be leaving immediately, if you will forgive my haste! It will be a pleasure doing business with you!"

"...Yep, thanks. Get home safe."

Alice lightly bobs her head as the beaming messenger bows deeply and leaves the room.

Once the messenger is out of sight, Alice murmurs softly to herself.

"...Guess that's all thanks to Lady Belial."

"Are you sure you're grateful? You look a little troubled. Are you perhaps regretting calling her here? Even just a little bit?"

At my prodding, Alice smiles.

"I'm glad to have you as a partner. You can share my concerns. Since you've known her for so long, do you mind if I ask you about her?"

"Go on."

Alice grabs my arm and asks me with a small smile on her lips:

"Having left in pursuit of the monsters, how many countries do you think Lady Belial will terrorize along the way? Just for reference, Grand Doble, the country we just entered into a friendly trade relationship with, was on the list of potential enemy states. You don't need me to tell you why, do you? ...What is it, partner? Don't be like that! I'm not letting you run away under these circumstances!"

"Lemme go, partner! This is all due to your whole secrecy schtick! If you'd kept me clued in, we could've avoided all of this from the start!"

After we finish trying to shift blame onto each other for a while, we sigh as we realize we've just wasted a lot of time.

"Given how much the messenger was groveling, I wonder what she did there. Honestly, I was too scared to ask."

"Did you know? Grand Doble is a great power that converted an inhospitable ancient ruin into a fortress city and has refused to bow to anyone's whims. Lady Belial forced a country like that to come to us, begging for a good relationship. She must have done something truly terrifying..."

Stop, I don't want to hear any more!

"But Grand Doble's supposed to be beyond the lands of even the old Demon Lord Realms. Just how did she stumble into there? I figured she'd be wandering around the woods..."

"Lady Belial's got more initiative and drive than just about anyone I know. Let's go by game terms: Assume a NEET can do one action per day. We Combat Agents can do five actions per day. In comparison, Lady Belial can do something like one hundred actions a day. Essentially, she can do the work of a hundred NEETs."

"Your analogy is so bad that it's hard to tell if I'm supposed to be impressed or not."

Well, either way, I'm glad she managed to make it out of the woods.

Alice looks a bit more relaxed, so she must feel the same way.

"Well, now we have an idea of the general area where she might be. I have no idea what she's done, but she did something big enough to make a country send a messenger in a panic. Let's send in a search party while Lady Belial's resting in Grand Doble."

I know then and there that Alice's remark has just jinxed us to failure...

[Three Days Since Belial's Disappearance]

We ignored the complaints that the return trip would take far longer than the initial trip and sent a bunch of agents through the teleporter to Grand Doble. Unfortunately, this search party was also unable to find Belial.

After the expendables asked around locally, we learned that Belial had incinerated a giant monster that was attacking the fortress wall, taking a piece of the wall with it, and told the authorities to send the repair bill to Kisaragi before vanishing.

"We don't have to worry about the repair fees. When the agent on the ground said, 'You were lucky it was just a piece of the fortress. If Lady Belial had used her full firepower, you could have lost the whole thing. So anyway, how much did you need?' they said we didn't have to worry about the cost."

"Why are our guys always so quick to try to pick a fight? Why can't we have the occasional tactful agent?"

I can't help but grumble when Alice, lying on my bed, looks intently at me, as though wanting to say something. Why?

...Just then, I hear a pounding of feet and a loud bang as my door is thrown open, and another expendable agent enters in a panic.

"Hey! They've confirmed a high-energy surge and huge shock waves in the northwest tundra! That's gotta be Lady Belial!"

"Seriously?" Alice can't help but sputter in shock, then, regaining her composure, calls out orders to the expendable.

"The tundra's at least a three days' drive from Grand Doble. Just how did she get there without so much as a bicycle? ...Well, never mind that. At least now we know where she is. This time, we'll get her with the teleporter...," Alice says to herself, forced to accept the illogical logic of Belial's route.

"Hey, Six, let's make a bet. Do you think Lady Belial will sit there and wait for the short amount of time it takes us to gather a search party and teleport them to that location?"

"Of course not. I'm wagering she'll be long gone by then."

I get into an argument about how unfair the bet is with the expendable while Alice just quietly stares at us.

* * *

[Four Days Since Belial's Disappearance]

Our effort at teleporting expendables to the tundra ended in failure.

When the expendables arrived, all they found was a field littered with the charred husks of countless monsters.

A search of the surrounding area revealed no sign of Belial, and the expendables on the ground indicated by radio that they couldn't even figure out what direction she had run off in.

To not even find a hint as to where she could have gone… This is why expendables are so useless…

When I tell them to turn back and come home, they start whining that they don't have enough points to order a vehicle and start begging for us to pick them up, so I decide to just cut the line.

Yes, right now finding Belial is a much higher priority than picking up a couple of Combat Agents.

Unfortunately, we don't have any clues, so the most we can do is just hurry up and wait here in the Hideout.

The day after I deploy the agents, I sit there watching Savage A do a strange dance at the Bashin tribe's temporary village…

<Notice for Combat Agent Six! A high-energy surge believed to be Lady Belial has been observed! Currently there are only two other Combat Agents left in the hideout! We have to hurry up and send one through the teleporter, but neither is answering their comms! I don't care which one you pick, go grab one and bring him here!>

The constant calls for help by the deployed agents have gotten so annoying that all of the agents left in Hideout City have their radios turned off.

Because of that, Alice isn't able to reach anyone by radio and has to resort to using the PA system.

There's a faint hint of frustration in Alice's voice as her announcement rings throughout Hideout City.

* * *

[Five Days Since Belial's Disappearance]

I drag a crying expendable to the teleporter. I get that he's short on Evil Points, but orders are orders. After we send him through the teleporter, we learn that Belial's already flown the coop.

When the expendable arrived, he found a group of lizardmen trembling as they stared wordlessly at a giant smoking crater.

According to the expendable's interviews, the crater is the result of a red-haired woman picking a fight with a raging god.

The lizardman village is apparently situated a little bit away from the crater, and they have to provide this raging god with a sacrifice once a year.

It's a pretty common trope in video games and fantasy novels, but evidently it piqued Belial's curiosity, and she asked the lizardmen to take her to the area where they encountered the raging god.

The raging god, upon seeing Belial, said, "This year's sacrifice has some fight in her, it seems."

To which she responded, "I'll be taking over as the raging god starting today. That makes *you* the sacrifice." She then proceeded to incinerate the god and just ran off into the distance.

The lizardmen, having watched the event unfold from start to finish, have started worshipping Belial as the new raging god… And that was around the time I grew bored of the report and hung up.

It's all well and good that we have lizardmen who owe us, but it's long past time we found Belial.

This is all the fault of the expendables running away when I tried to catch them and teleport them. If they'd just reported to the teleporter when we detected the energy surge, we might have found her.

But this time, we've accounted for that problem.

"Hey, Alice, why am I the one getting sent off next?! Since Six is still here, why don't we settle this with a coin toss?!"

"Shut up! I'm the ace in the hole, so I can't go off on random errands like this! Besides, for whatever reason, I get Evil Points every time we teleport you. It's important to make sure I have enough points to deal with any unforeseen complications."

I lightly pat the expendable's shoulder, even as he struggles against the wire that restrains him.

"Screw that! None of the agents that have been sent out have come back yet! At the very least, give me some equipment before you send me off! Hey! Don't push!"

I shove the whining expendable into the teleporter, when I come to a realization.

"Hey, Alice, I bet it'll be too late if we wait to detect an energy surge. We should try to guess the next explosion point and send him on ahead."

"That's pretty smart coming from you. Good plan, we'll go with that."

"Don't go with it! I mean, Six is one thing, but Alice, think it through a bit more!"

Alice and I ignore the expendable as he continues to whine and complain, and we spread out a map to guess the next explosion point.

Alice seriously thinks over the possibilities, but I decide to just stand a pencil up on the map and let it fall on a random spot.

"My guess is here. It's my gut instinct as the most senior surviving Combat Agent. She's probably almost certainly there."

"I think it's more likely to be near this city-state. But I guess we should go with your gut as a Combat Agent."

"You idiot! A random pencil drop's got nothing to do with your gut, dammit! The city-state! Please send me to the city-state!"

As the expendable continues to make demands, I give him the bare minimum equipment of a pack of Calorie-Z bars and water.

"When they sent me to this rock, they used a roll of the dice to choose me! Quit being such a baby and go already!"

"Hey, wait, at least untie me..."

I press the teleport button before the expendable finishes his sentence, immediately hearing the Evil Point chime in my head. That instant, the observation monitor lights up when the sensors detect another energy surge.

The dot indicates a spot near the city-state, which means…

"I guess even a Combat Agent's gut instinct fails every now and then. Don't worry about it; let's do better next time."

"Hey, Alice. Aren't you starting to enjoy this a bit?"

[Six Days Since Belial's Disappearance]

"The agent we sent out randomly yesterday has made his way to the city-state on his own. Since it's a good opportunity, I'm having him report on the Belial situation while establishing diplomatic relations."

"Then I guess it's a big win after all. Good to see him doing his job properly."

Alice and I exchange nods in the teleporter room.

"So we're now out of Combat Agents to teleport…"

"That's fine. Since you're not as strong as Combat Agents, we'll be sending you two as a pair."

We look toward the platform where Snow and Heine are tied up with wire.

"What are you talking about?! Wait, is the reason there's no Combat Agents in Hideout City…?"

"Hold up, if you send the two of us into a place we've never been, of course we're not going to make it back alive!"

The two wail even as they struggle against their restraints, but we've prepared supplies for these two.

"Water and rations, tent and radio. Map, matches, and a compass… Am I forgetting anything?"

"No, that should be more than enough. If you give them too much, it won't be good survival training."

...Survival training?

"What do you mean training? I'm the greatest knight in the kingdom! I don't need any training!"

"I used to be a commander in the Demon Lord Army! What's the point of making me do this training?!"

Alice shakes her head in feigned exasperation.

"We've all been getting a bit soft from a lack of activity. Since the Combat Agents have been losing to monsters, it's time to remind them just how harsh an environment this world can be."

"That has nothing to do with me! I'm a knight, but I'm more of a strategist than a grunt!"

"Th-then, so am I... *Sniff...sob...*"

"You two aren't that much smarter than I am."

Well, Snow and Heine aside, I guess Alice wasn't just enjoying teleporting people off into random areas.

It's true that the harsh environment of this world makes it perfect for survival training. That's why she's the brains of our operation...

"Right, let's send you two to the Midgard Mountains, where the dragons are supposed to live. Dragons are fire monsters. I'm sure you'll be happy to join more of your kind, Heine."

"Wait, the Midgard Mountains are waaay too far away! That's not the sort of distance for a training mission!"

"Even if we use the same element, I don't feel any kinship with dragons! Wait, hang—"

...Alice presses the button, even as I admire the thought she's put into the whole operation.

"Anyway, the Midgard Mountains only have greater dragons. Those sorts are intelligent, so they probably can't be bothered to attack people. The first batch of Combat Agents should be getting back soon. Where should I send them next?"

"...Yeah, you're definitely enjoying this."

* * *

[And now…]

Over the past few days, we've had a constant stream of messengers declaring their country or city's submission to Kisaragi, but yesterday, we didn't encounter any sign of Belial.

Instead, we got a messenger from Grunade today.

Yes, the same Grunade that had its national treasure, a giant sorcery stone, stolen by a bipedal feline monster.

"Did they figure out that Tiger Man is one of ours? Are we going to war?"

"No. While they might be suspecting our involvement, I doubt they have any solid evidence. That gives us some wiggle room. We told them that the Hiiragi Agency of Order has its own giant feline monster, remember? Maybe they just want to learn the details."

So the game plan is to hear what they have to say, then decide whether to go on the offensive, or simply apologize.

After confirming our plan of action, Alice and I invite the messenger into the room.

[Intermission 2] —My First Memory of Meeting Him—

"Let me ask again. What did that boy say?"

My mind feels fuzzy, and I answer Lilith as she peers down at me.

The first thing the new part-timer said to me was, "Miss Yukari, your boobs are huge. What'd you eat to get them that big?"

"Well, he's starting off on the wrong note right there," the girl says as she writes something down in a notebook.

"Um, and then what? Did the boy say anything else?"

At her urging, I continue to search my memory...

I think he said... "I'm the prince of the planet Booba, and I need to have boobies placed on my head on a regular basis or I'll die. So can you help me out?"

"Hmm... That's even worse."

...That's right. I've never liked these big breasts. They've been nothing but a backache ever since I was in school.

All the boys in class would make fun of my body and bully me because of it.

When I told the new boy about that, he said, "That's the sort of thing brats do when they like a girl but are too shy to say it. It just means all those jerks liked you a lot, Miss Yukari." I remember him lying to me to make me feel better...

"If you keep telling me about his misdeeds, I'm going to have to dock his pay. But, then again, it seems like your memories involving him are the ones that are easiest to recover..."

...That reminds me, I've always had an inferiority complex about being really tall.

Which is why I got into the habit of hunching down to try and make myself look smaller...

"All right, here's a few more questions. What's the most memorable thing that boy told you?"

…The most memorable thing?

He smiled as he pointed out that I was always hunching over.

He smacked me on the back to make me straighten up and looked up at me with a smile.

"You need to go around with your head held high, Miss Yukari. It's such a waste!"

Then he continued.

"You've got these awesome assets! You should puff out your chest more and really show off those milkers! The superheroes won't stand a chance, then…"

"You're the worst!!"

CHAPTER 3

Vs. Tiger Man!

1

One day after we sent the messenger from Grunade home.

"Nope, nope, nope! I'm still recovering from fighting that dragon! There's no way I'm going to Grunade!"

The two convalescent chimeras don't seem super happy about their next destination.

"Hey, Combat Agent apprentice! In Kisaragi, we follow orders! Tantrums don't get you off from work! When I say you're going, that's that!"

"That's not true, Boss! You never listen to anything Ms. Viper says!"

Rose is offering more resistance than usual, but unfortunately for her, we're short on manpower.

"That's different. I've gone so deep into the dark side that insubordination's just a part of me. Besides, it's hard for me to think of Vi as my boss."

"Th-then, I've fallen to the dark side, too! Just yesterday, I took Little Bashin's snack for myself!"

Oh, so that's why Little Bashin was chasing her around yesterday.

Russell, watching our exchange wearily, speaks up.

"Hey, Six, can you at least fill us in on what happened while we were hurt?"

"Yeah! Isn't Grunade the country where Mr. Tiger Man caused a huge incident?! If a messenger came from there, and we're heading that way, that must mean…!"

Alice smiles reassuringly at Rose, trying to set her concerns to rest.

"Yeah, we got an official messenger from Grunade yesterday. They heard we took down the Demon Lord's Army, so they've asked us to send some of our Combat Agents."

Right now, the countries in this region seem to think of us as a mercenary army on retainer with the Grace Kingdom.

Since deploying Combat Agents for hire is a core part of our business, we were more than happy to take Grunade's business.

"…Grunade has an army, right? So why would they come asking for our help?"

Evidently, making her do elementary school lessons is having the undesirable side effect of making Rose less gullible.

Alice continues to smile reassuringly at her.

"See, the feline monster that took Grunade's national treasure ran off into the forest, and it seems that monster's really good at fighting in woodlands. They heard we've succeeded in settling the cursed woods, so they decided we'd be the right people for the job."

"…I see, so we're going to make it look like we took back the sorcery stone from Tiger Man and take their money? Y'know, Boss, it seems like you guys spend a lot of time getting paid to put out fires you started."

I look at Rose with a sad expression in response to her caustic commentary.

"Rose… When I first met you, you were less jaded, loyal to your friends, and brave despite your small size, but you've changed. I mean,

I get it, we suspected that Tiger Man was the sorcery stone thief. But it hasn't been proven yet. Even if the possibility is slim, Alice and I will continue to believe in our friend."

"Well said, Six. That's right, Kisaragi may be an evil corporation, but we value our comrades. We have to keep the faith when no one else will."

"I might not be very smart, but this little act is too obviously fake, even for me. Seriously, all you need to do is convince Tiger Man to return the sorcery stone. Then there's no need for us to go along with you, is there?"

Since Rose is looking at us with suspicion, I decide it's time to abandon the subterfuge.

"Fine! You're right, the plan is to get the sorcery stone from Tiger Man and make Grunade owe us a favor. This is a huge opportunity for easy money. Because an entire country is offering the job, the reward is huge."

"Yep, the reason we're taking you is to have sacrifices in case Tiger Man throws a tantrum about giving back the sorcery stone. He has a weakness for lolis, after all."

As we quickly admit to our scheme, Rose and Russell snap back.

"What do you mean sacrifices? What are you planning to make us do?"

"If that's the reason, I'm not going! If you need a loli, Alice should be enough!"

Tiger Man can be a handful to deal with.

While he likes Alice, he doesn't automatically listen to what she says because she's not an organic loli.

"Alice, let's just restrain them and teleport them. Get me some steel wire."

"It's true that that'll be faster. I'll go fetch Viper. Take that time to tie them up."

Alice orders the steel wire then leaves the room. At her exit, the remaining two chimeras raise their hackles.

"You're forcing us to go?! You're the worst, Boss! W-what? Are you going to try it?! There's two of us, so we're not going to lose to you, Boss!"

"You're definitely underestimating combat chimeras. Do you really think a mere human can beat us head-to-head?"

I ready the steel wire in one hand, then toss my anti-chimera secret weapon into the air.

"Here's that luxury snack from Earth you wanted to try, Rose. Oh, by the way, there's only one."

"Hyah!"

Rose locks on to the treat and pounces on it.

"H-hey, Rose, what are you doing?! That can wait until later! Focus on taking Six out first!"

"Rose, as I said, there's only one serving of the snack. Even if you beat me by cooperating with Russell, you'll have to fight over the snack once that's done. Get what I'm saying?"

Rose firmly grasps the snack and casts a suspicious glance at Russell.

"R-Rose? I don't want the snack, and you have no need to be wary of me."

Russell seems taken aback even as he tries to persuade Rose, but I launch a follow-up attack.

"Hey, Rose, is there any guarantee that he won't just take the snack from you after you're exhausted from fighting me? As Russell's quick to point out, you and he are both chimeras. As a chimera, can you *really* believe another chimera when they say they don't want the snack?"

Rose's eyes go wide in understanding as she leaps away from Russell.

"I can't…trust him… It's impossible that a combat chimera would give up on having a luxury snack that's not from this world…"

"It is possible!! Which reminds me, would you stop trying to ruin the reputation of combat chimeras?! I'm not a slave to my hunger like you are!"

Russell pleads with Rose, even as she is fully on guard for any treachery from him.

I circle around behind Russell, wire in hand.

"Also, since that luxury snack 'chule' isn't for humans, I won't eat it. Meaning, if you cooperate with me to take down Russell, you're guaranteed to have the chule all to yourself. Now, choose! Will you side with the ex–Demon Lord's Army cross-dressing chimera? Or me, the comrade you've fought alongside for ages?!"

"I know Kisaragi is an evil organization, but you value your comrades, right? Then it's an easy choice. After all, I'm a Combat Agent apprentice of the Kisaragi Corporation, Rose the combat chimera!"

"Okay, we're definitely not cousins. Chimeras aren't *this* stupid!" yells Russell tearfully, as Rose and I pounce on him from both sides.

As I stand waiting in front of the teleporter, Alice and Viper enter the room.

"Yo, Six. Good job. Looks like you're all set."

"Yep, we're ready when you are. Okay, Vi, we're trusting you to teleport us safely and defend the hideout as well."

The bound and gagged chimeras inside the teleporter pod raise their voices through their gags as though they're trying to object.

Ordinarily, we'd prefer to take Viper along as well, but Hideout City is suffering from a serious Combat Agent shortage at the moment, so we need to keep her here as a reserve in case of an emergency.

I shouldn't have been so cavalier about sending off the others, even if they were a good source of Evil Points.

Viper, having been educated on how to operate the teleporter by Alice, then turns to look at us.

"Mr. Six, Grunade is currently in the middle of an intense succession battle after the sudden passing of its king. Please try to avoid getting dragged into the conflict…," she says with a hint of worry in her voice.

Honestly, she sounds like she's setting up a death flag…

"It'll be fine, Vi. This is already a done deal. We'll ignore all of that drama, get the job done, then hightail it outta the country. So don't worry and just look forward to the souvenirs we're gonna bring you."

"Yeah, I'll make sure to keep a close eye on things. There won't be any problems. I'm leaving Hideout City in your capable hands."

Viper still looks anxious, but she nods at our reassuring words.

"Mmrrmph!"

"Faiffer! Faifferr heeelf!"

We step into the teleportation pod to make our way to Grunade.

2

"Hey, Alice, are those baby dragons? This country's people sure keep some dangerous pets."

"They don't have any wings, so they're more like lizards than dragons. I hear dragon worship is all the rage in Grunade, so I guess they worship dragon-like creatures as well."

Having been teleported into Grunade, Alice and I tossed Rose and Russell into a room of the inn we'll be using as our base of operations before heading out to the city to do some scouting.

There's a lot of lizards that resemble Komodo dragons wandering around the city. The owner of a fruit shop tosses some of the fruit he sells to a lizard that approaches his store.

Being located at the foot of a mountain range, they seem to have a great deal more water than the wastelands around the Grace Kingdom, and the city seems a lot more prosperous as a result.

The Midgard Mountains that we can see from the city are devoid of any trees. I wonder if that's because they've already cleared them for lumber.

The architecture and fashion styles don't seem all that different from Grace or Torace.

As we observe the people coming and going along the streets, Alice speaks to me in Japanese.

"<There's more people here than in Grace. Plus, there's a decent number of men since they haven't been fighting a war. The city's protected by a giant wall, so it looks like this country would be a pain to invade.>"

"<I guess that's why the Demon Lord Army went after Grace instead. That, and they were closer.>"

Based on the fact that none of the city's residents seem bothered by us chatting in Japanese, they probably have pretty extensive trade relations with other countries as well.

After peering at the wares offered at various shops, Alice tilts her head quizzically.

"For a country so close to the mountains, there aren't a lot of stores that deal in metal and stone. Usually, mountain ranges are rich in mineral resources, but maybe they already exhausted all of the veins? Otherwise, I doubt they'd build a city in a place like this."

"Maybe it's built around an artifact as well? The city of Grace in the Grace Kingdom was built where it is now because they couldn't move the rainmaking artifact."

Cities and countries on this planet tend to be built near ancient ruins or artifacts.

So it wouldn't be surprising if the same was true of Grunade.

"I'd be interested in looking into whether there's an artifact or not. I've also been researching sorcery stones, but there's way too much about them that makes no sense. Once we get our business finished, it'd be good to take some time to do a survey."

"Not to jinx us, but this job would be super easy. There's still the matter of the missing Lady Belial to deal with, so let's get this cake-walk over with!"

After hearing the assignment from the employer, I have to ask them to repeat themselves.

"Excuse me, can you say that again?"

We're in a receiving room in Grunade castle.

Having finished our scouting disguised as tourists, we've come to the castle to get our easy little job out of the way.

"The assignment is to retrieve the national treasure from the feline monster lurking in the forest. We do not care if the feline monster is alive or dead, but we can offer you an additional reward if you kill it."

The middle-aged butler-like man begins explaining the assignment again.

The woman in her early twenties standing next to him and looking over at us appraisingly is evidently this kingdom's first princess, Christopher Lydia Grunade.

She has long blond hair, strong blue eyes, and the air of a ruler.

So far there's no problem with the assignment.

The fact that they don't care about the feline monster's state is fine for us since we have no intention of fighting Tiger Man.

The problem is…

"The feline monster who stole our national treasure also kidnapped the young second princess of the kingdom and retreated into the woods, and he continues to attack anyone who enters them. Our knights aren't used to fighting in forested terrain, which is why we have been forced to swallow our pride and ask for help from you, the Kisaragi Corporation."

That's the moment when Tiger Man blew past the line that should never be crossed.

* * *

He's finally done it.

Ordinarily, I'd suspect he didn't actually do it, but I can't possibly defend him after learning that the second princess is a young girl.

Even as I'm struggling to contain my unease, Alice responds with a perfect professional smile.

"I understand. We will accept this assignment. We'll do whatever is necessary to eliminate the feline monster."

"Huh? No, eliminating the feline monster is secondary but… V-very well."

Yes. The hard rule in Kisaragi is that going after children gets you the death penalty.

Alice is completely committed to dealing with Tiger Man, and her determination seems to cow the butler, who simply nods, prompting the princess to speak.

"You seem to have your doubts about the situation."

"… …? …Huh? You mean me?"

I'm taken aback as she directs her comment at me, and the princess responds with a faint smile and a cold gaze.

"You don't need to try to hide it. I'm sure you're wondering why we haven't brought up the rescue of the kidnapped second princess, yes?"

Actually, I'm just shocked because one of my comrades has become a serious sex offender.

…As I'm trying to find the words to express this, the princess smiles self-deprecatingly.

"You are aware of what is going on in this country, yes? That the faction backing me, the first princess, and the faction backing my younger brother, the first prince, are fighting over the crown due to my father's sudden passing."

Sorry, I didn't know that.

The princess seems to take my silence as acknowledgment and continues with a wintry smile.

"I'm the one who was given the responsibility of managing the national treasure. This country doesn't function without that sorcery stone. If the elder daughter who has the strongest claim to the throne loses the national treasure *and* her rival, the prince recovers it, and it's clear who will have the strongest claim to the throne, isn't it? Meaning…the one behind all of this is my brother."

Sorry, I'm pretty sure that's not it at all.

"Considering how sentimental he can be, he's thought this one through pretty well. If he ruins my reputation and proclaims he recovered the national treasure, then the throne is as good as his. The reason he kidnapped our younger sister was to make sure there weren't any loose ends, since she has a claim to the throne as well. I thought he wouldn't risk hurting her, but…"

I'm pretty sure not a single hair on your sister's head has been harmed.

"Simply put, there's no reason why a monster would come and steal something they can't eat like a sorcery stone, especially when it's heavily guarded. Then there's the fact that there were plenty of more appetizing people around, but the monster chose to abduct my young sister instead. Why? All of this only makes sense if my brother is the one who sent that beast."

I'm sorry, we can actually provide an alternative explanation that makes perfect sense.

"Still, I wasn't able to ascertain how my brother was able to control the monster. That makes it impossible to accuse him of the crime… But then we received this letter."

The princess glances over to the butler, who takes a letter out of his fob and spreads it on the table.

"This is a note from the Grace Kingdom. It speaks of how an organization calling itself the Hiiragi Agency of Order, which has conquered the Torace Kingdom, sent a feline monster to attack the Grace Kingdom."

"Indeed, that was quite the incident. They came out of nowhere and started causing massive problems in the city."

"Yeah, and one of our officers, a woman named Viper, was seriously injured in the process."

The princess's expression sours further as Alice and I follow up on the letter's contents.

"You see, there's actually a representative who claims to be from the Hiiragi Agency of Order here in this country as we speak—"

3

Alice and I stand in front of the conference room door in the Grunade Palace before I kick open the door and stomp our way inside.

"All right! Come on out, Adelie! What the hell are you doing here?!"

"Pbbt!"

As we barge into the conference room, Adelie suddenly spews the tea she was drinking across the place.

Inside, a silver-haired young man who was discussing something with her sits frozen in shock, while the knights guarding him place their hands on the hilts of their swords, ready to deal with any potential threats.

"Agentsix?! W-what are YOU doing here?!"

Adelie wipes the tea from her chin with a handkerchief and stands up.

"We're Combat Agents, so it should be obvious. We've been hired to go retrieve the national treasure that's been taken by the feline monster."

"We can ask the same of you. This your next conquest after Torace? The princess mentioned you and all the dark rumors surrounding your arrival."

Adelie hurriedly responds in a panic to our sudden accusations.

"T-that's not it at all! Since we were about to be blamed for the feline monster stealing the sorcery stone, I came here to prove our innocence!"

"T-that's right! When our messenger communicated the precarious state of Grunade due to the theft of the treasure, Dame Adelheid volunteered to come and help retrieve the national treasure from the monster! For some reason, my elder sister Lydia believes I'm behind the theft, but I swear that it isn't me!"

The one who follows up on Adelie's testimony is the young man who was discussing something with her.

This must be Lydia's younger brother.

"But, Your Highness. She was responsible for all sorts of villainy in the Grace Kingdom. She claimed she was a servant of justice and started enforcing laws as a vigilante. And because she let a giant feline monster loose, our virtuous superior was badly injured."

"Yep, and we're told your second princess has been kidnapped. That woman there has a history of trying to kidnap a boy."

Hearing our accusations, the prince looks worriedly up at Adelie.

"...Dame Adelheid?"

"N-n-n-n-no, that's...! Well, it's true, but it's not true! Yes, what they're saying is true, but there's a deep reason behind all of it!"

We know better than anyone that she's actually innocent.

"Hey, Miss Adelie of the long rap sheet! You seem pretty cozy with the prince's supporters, but this is what we call good old-fashioned political meddling!"

"Careful, Your Highness. They've got a history of knocking off royals. Just look at what they did to Torace. The moment you're on the throne, they're probably going to start demanding payment for their support."

"..."

"Please wait, Prince Madia! Don't go all quiet on me! You were the one who sent a messenger to our agency regarding the feline monster! We had no idea that anything like that had happened until you sent us your message! You can use the lie detector crystal on me if you wish!"

At Adelie's plea, the prince—Madia—seems to return to his senses.

"T-that's right. According to the messenger who met with Dame Adelheid, she acted with utter shock, as though the news had hit her like a bolt from the blue..."

"They can say whatever they want. And it's pretty easy to fool lie detectors. There's plenty of ways for them to play dumb if they want to."

Alice continues to stir the pot, prompting Adelie to produce an object and place it on the table.

"Hiiragi Agency of Order Crystal Series number two! The crystal of truth!"

I poke the crystal ball Adelie put on the table, making it roll around.

"I've seen something like this before. I remember seeing a magic device that would chime *ding-dong* when someone lied."

"I'll explain, so listen to me! This works on the same principles as the karma-measuring orb. If the words are false, the crystal ball turns black. I'll try it out first, so you try lying!"

Desperate to convince the prince that she's telling the truth, Adelie enthusiastically places her hand on the orb.

"Please believe me, Your Highness. I have no involvement with the monster that took your national treasure. And I really am here to prove my innocence."

As Adelie makes her earnest declaration while looking the prince in the eye, the orb begins to glow a bright white.

"Dame Adelheid...you've done enough. I will trust you. Ahm... While I appreciate you two coming to warn me..."

Before the prince can finish, Alice and I put our hands on the orb.

"I'm actually a modified human from a really distant planet here to invade and conquer this world."

"I'm something like a golem created by the hand of a human being and I'm not even human. If I take heavy damage, I'll self-destruct and reduce the area round me into a burnt-out wasteland, so be careful how you handle me."

At our ridiculous statements, the orb continues to shine brightly.

"...Y-you two... You're not lying... Is that the truth...?"

Seeing the orb shimmering, Adelie and the prince gulp down a breath.

"Despite the fact that I'm supposed to be on a mission to save all of humanity, I'm just a rank-and-file employee on a super-low salary being used and abused. What I'm really good at is stuffing peanuts into my nose, then blowing them right where I'm aiming."

"My special skill is calculating pi to the eighty-trillionth place within a minute. Among the members sent to invade this planet is a weirdo who tries to poop in a princess's room and, when sent on an infiltration mission, takes a bath in the enemy commander's room and relaxes in their bedroom..."

"Dame Adelheid, this orb is broken."

"Th-that's not it. They're probably telling the truth... No, that's impossible, isn't it? I'm sorry!"

With doubt cast on the orb's effectiveness, Adelie looks on the verge of tears as she pleads her case.

As the prince gazes at Adelia with skepticism, she shoots a pleading glance over at us for help.

Evidently struck by Adelie's entreating look, Alice sighs and responds.

"Hey, Adelie, where I come from, there's a saying that the just always win. Given that you love to wail on and on about justice, if you really are a servant of justice, prove it by beating us. Whoever takes back the national treasure from the feline monster is the winner and righteous. It's nice in its simplicity, isn't it?"

"...I see. We'll face off to prove who's right! I like it! I really like it!"

Alice's proposal is the sort of thing that's common in shonen manga series, but it seems to have struck a chord with Adelie as well.

"I'm sure you've got terms you want fulfilled if you win, right? Awful, scandalous terms that I can't possibly accept, maybe something gross or filthy...!"

Adelie hugs herself and backs away.

"Then...when we win, can we judge you to be evil and execute you?"

"Of course not! Can't you come up with something a little nicer?!"

Alice chimes in, sounding like a villain trying to force unreasonable terms on the main character.

4

After returning to the inn, we recap the events in the castle to the still-restrained chimeras.

"So things have changed. The target we're going to eliminate is an ex–Kisaragi Corporation leader, the lolicon mutant Tiger Man. No restrictions on methods. Do whatever it takes to eliminate him."

"Um, I'm sorry Miss Alice, I don't understand what you're saying."

"Um...did he really do something that serious? Maybe there's a reason behind it?"

The two chimeras appear troubled by our explanation.

"In Kisaragi, you're executed the moment you do something to children. I know you two like Tiger Man, but you two know what he's like, right?"

"I always thought Tiger Man would cross that line eventually.

Just a few weeks ago, he was asking the Kisaragi Corporation's Legal Counsel whether crimes committed on another planet were actually subject to Earth's laws."

Despite our efforts at persuasion, the two who have been thoroughly brainwashed by Tiger Man's honeyed cunning continue to protest.

"Aren't you guys Tiger Man's friends? At least try to have a little more faith in him. Why can't we settle this by talking it out?"

"That's right. Whatever else he might be, Tiger Man's a gentleman when it comes to children. Besides, we don't stand a chance against him. Russell is right; we should start by trying to talk to him."

Our opponent is Tiger Man, one of the most powerful of the mutants. Without the help of the chimeras, the odds are definitely against us.

Alice and I swap glances, then exchange nods.

"If you two insist, then I guess we don't have much choice. Let's assume that Tiger Man is doing this for a reason and start off by talking to him."

"*Tch*, we're going to try it your way just this once, guys."

As we shrug in surrender, Rose and Russell smile.

"<—To the sex offender, mutant Tiger Man hiding in the woods! Surender peacefully, and we'll execute you painlessly via lethal injection! If you won't, we'll execute you after handing you over to the punishment squadron!>"

Alice spends an hour broadcasting in Japanese over a loudspeaker into the woods near Grunade.

With his sharp ears, Tiger Man should've heard her by now…

"Hey, Alice, there's no sign of him. We should move on to plan B soon."

"Fair enough. It seems Tiger Man has no intention of engaging in negotiations. We've done everything we can. I think we've kept our promise to Rose and Russell."

"Do you two intend to claim that those broadcasts constitute negotiating?"

Since he's not responding to our entreaties, it's time to shift to a more forceful plan of action.

"So now it's time for Russell to do some work."

"Mmmph! Mmmrrmph! Mrrph!"

Russell, who's been tied up this whole time, starts whining through his gag.

"Lolis are Tiger Man's weakness. We tried your request to talk to him first. Now it's time for you guys to listen to our request."

"Don't worry, he'll come. Plan B will work."

"Phiph iphn't phephophiaphing!"

Russell shakes his head trying to protest, but Alice resumes broadcasting through the loudspeaker.

"<To the fugitive Tiger Man! We currently have the loli chimeras in our custody! If you don't come out now, we'll force Russell to work in a groping-allowed maid café!>"

<Evil Points Acquired>

As I rejoice in my newly acquired Evil Points while sitting next to Alice, Rose backs away a few steps, frowning.

"I don't know what Miss Alice is saying, but it's probably nothing good."

"I told you, we're going to have Russell do some work. We're just going to make him work in a café. Tiger Man happens to be as possessive of his targets as Mutant Bear Woman…"

Just then:

Something's thrown at our feet.

I close my eyes, grab Alice, and leap to the side as a loud bang is followed by a bright flash.

"Ack! My eyes!"

Rose screams something, covering her face with both hands and rolling around in pain, but the flash bang's deafened me, so I can't make out what she's saying.

A large object leaps out from the depths of the forest toward us.

From my arms, Alice aims her shotgun and fires as the object heads straight for us.

The object, aka Tiger Man, just covers his face and continues closing in on us, shrugging off the shotgun pellets.

I keep hold of Alice in one arm, while drawing my pistol with the other!

"Don't move!"

<Evil Points Acquired>

I press the barrel into Russell, who thrashes around in his restraints in agony from the stun grenade.

Tiger Man, who's always had a soft spot for Russell, comes to a halt and murmurs.

"...Mrreow, that's low. Rrrrussell's alwaysss cooked and cleaned for you all this trrrime."

"My ears are ringing so I can't hear what you're saying."

Alice, who's crawled down from my arms, takes out a single syringe and approaches Tiger Man.

"All right, don't resist, Tiger Man. I'll at least make sure you don't suffer."

"I've always liked your sssspunk, Mreowlice. But execution without even questioning is a bit mrruch."

As my hearing returns, I glance toward Alice as she sidles toward Tiger Man and ask:

"Tiger Man, why did you do this? What happened to the spirit of 'yes to Lolitas, no to touching'? At least go out with a bit of dignity at the very end, please."

"Prrrroperly Kisarrrragi. Coming to kill meeee without meowasking any questions and without hesitation. Before I continue, I swearrr I haven't done anything illegal to Nyowdia."

Actually, I'm pretty sure kidnapping is a serious and illegal offense.

"Just what are you lot doing herrrere meoanyway? Whrrat happened to purrrotecting and building the city?"

"We're here because you screwed up big time, Tiger Man. They hired us to come and hunt down the feline monster. At the very least, can you return the national treasure and the princess you kidnapped?"

Since he seems to have no intention of fighting, I urge him to cooperate, and I holster my pistol, but Tiger Man flatly refuses.

"Nyope!"

Alice silently throws the syringe at him, but Tiger Man easily dodges it.

"Stop being such a pain in the ass, you goddamned pedo! If you don't want us to call Kisaragi's punishment squad, at least hand over the damned sorcery stone!"

I know we were told the priority was recovering the national treasure, but why isn't the demand to return Princess Nadia first?

...Just then, Rose, who's been rolling around on the ground, shakily rises to her feet.

"I...don't think you're someone who'd arbitrarily kidnap a girl, Tiger Man. You have a reason for doing this, right?"

"When I went to steal the sorrrrccery sssstone, sshheee looked lll-looonely, so I breowught her home with mrreeeow."

Rose draws in a breath, then blows flames out toward Tiger Man.

As Tiger Man leaps back to avoid the fire, I propose a compromise.

"Tiger Man, listen to me, please. We're in the middle of competing with the Hiiragi Agency of Order to see who can be the one to bring back the national treasure, so can you just give it to us for the moment?"

"...Right. While I'd prefer to execute you, I'll settle for that. Once we've handed over the national treasure and taken the payment, you can steal it again or do whatever you want."

I mean, what we're saying is pretty damned awful, but we are, in the end, an evil corporation.

"I craaan't."

......

"Surround him. I'll order a boatload of those shady syringes and we'll all throw them at him at once."

"Crrrralm down and lisssten, Meowlice... I said I crran't, not that I won't... Because..."

Tiger Man produces something that looks like a jewel split in half from his pocket.

"The sorcery stone split when I handled it too rough. Mrr."

"The hell are you doing?!"

We decide to have a temporary cease-fire to figure out what to do, and we've gathered around the pieces of the sorcery stone lying on the ground.

"I tried gluing it together using superglue, but what'll we do about this?"

Alice, having repaired the sorcery stone, gazes intently at it and lightly pokes the spot she glued together.

The sorcery stone in front of us is red in color and about the size of two adult fists.

"At a glance, it doesn't look like it was ever broken in the first place. Maybe we can just get away with handing it over as it is?"

At that suggestion, Rose raises her hand with a proposal of her own.

"Why don't we just admit that the sorcery stone broke and prepare a replacement? Look, Russell's sorcery stone is pretty big since he's part of the Demon Lord Army's leadership..."

"Mrrrmph! Mrrm!"

As Russell tries to object through his gag to his fellow chimera's suggestion, Tiger Man shakes his head.

"From whrrat Nyowdia trrold me, the sorcery strrrone used in Gurrrrnade is special. Rrrrurrrssell's sorcery stone is a blue water stone, so it prrrobably can't be used as a substitute."

Tiger Man's words seem to jog Rose's memory about something else.

"Oh that reminds me, Tiger Man. What sort of life is Miss Nadia living right now? I mean, she's a princess. Isn't it hard for her to live out in the forest?"

"She's enjoying life in the trrrrailer home sent frrrom Kisaragi. She's rrrreeally happy with the food from Earrrth, and she was overwhelmed by the luxury desserts."

Rose lets out a sigh of relief then smiles.

"I see, then that's a relief… Speaking of which, since she's a princess, she probably needs an attendant or a bodyguard who's a woman, doesn't she? For example, I think I'd make a pretty good candidate."

"It's obvrrrrious Rrrrose just wants to eat delicious food. If I werrre to find an attendant, it'd be Rrurrssell, who can do chores."

A look of resignation comes to Russell's face as Tiger Man pulls the restrained chimera closer.

Just then…

"That's enough!"

Adelie appears in a flash of blue-white light, her foot emitting an energy aura as she unleashes a jump kick against Tiger Man.

She appeared out of thin air. Her armor must be equipped with optical camo.

Adelie's sneak attack appeared impossible to avoid, but Tiger Man somehow manages to block it by holding an object out as a shield.

With her sneak attack foiled, Adelie jumps backward and points her index finger accusingly at Tiger Man.

"Vile monster who kidnapped a young girl and is now trying to kidnap a young boy! I, Adelheid the Dark Gray Savior, Apostle of the Hiiragi Agency of Order, will fight you!"

I thought she might have listened in on our conversation while cloaked, but based on her attitude, it seems she's not aware of our relationship with Tiger Man.

"What the heck are you doing? Self-proclaimed heroes shouldn't be doing sneak attacks."

"Saving lives matters more than being honorable. I'll happily be called a knave if it means it saves a boy's life."

Adelie's bright smile is like a breath of fresh air...but everyone's attention is focused on something else...

"Oh, the sorcery stone's in tiny pieces now."

Adelie freezes at Rose's soft murmur.

"...No, you have the wrong idea. I was just trying to save the boy being held by the monster."

Oh, I see, she seems to think Tiger Man's the one who tied up Russell.

Well, true, Russell being tied up with metal wire and gagged looks all sorts of criminal, but...

"<Hey, Six. Who the hell is thrrris woman who appuurrred out of nowhere and shattered the sorcery strrone?>" Tiger Man asks in Japanese, but we can't have her learning that he's affiliated with Kisaragi.

As I struggle to figure out how to respond, Alice speaks up.

"We can punish Adelie later. Six, stun that feline monster with a flash bang."

"Got it. Monsters are vulnerable to loud noises and light. Hell, it might even be spooked off by the bang."

"<So you're saying I should flee into the woods when Srrrix throws the grrrrrenade?>" Tiger Man murmurs in Japanese while Alice and I talk to each other as though he can't understand human speech.

"I've heard this monster is strong, but maybe the two of us can take it down together? It's better to finish it off here than to scare it away and have it run back into the woods…"

As Adelie tries to put a dent in our plans, Tiger Man holds up Russell threateningly.

"Damn, with Russell as his hostage, we can't afford to attack him!"

"Oh… Oh no. If I attack the monster, something terrible might happen to Russell…"

"Are you telling us to sacrifice Russell?! Adelie, I thought you were better than that!"

Adelie hurriedly shakes her head in response to our bluffing.

"N-no, that's not it! Yes, we need to prioritize the boy's life! Okay! Let's go with your plan!"

I throw the flash bang before I even finish hearing Adelie's reply!

5

"…And so the feline monster kidnapped one of our companions to use as a hostage and escaped back into the woods. As for the all-important sorcery stone…"

Alice and I point our index fingers at the kowtowing Adelie.

"She shattered it."

"I'm very sorry! I'm very sorry! I'm truly, very sorry!"

Requesting a meeting with our employer, we're then brought into a receiving room…

"Oh, I see! One of my brother's collaborators destroyed the sorcery stone…? Oh my!"

"Mrrrrgh."

As Lydia smiles triumphantly at our report, the prince is holding back a groan of frustration.

Lydia, who is in the middle of a struggle for succession, must be overjoyed that the rival faction has committed such a costly error.

"See, I tried to tell you, Prince. This woman's nothing but trouble."

"Yo, why are you so damned useless?! Apologize, dammit! Say you're sorry for shattering the sorcery stone; say you're sorry for being born!"

"I'm sorry I was born! I'm sorry, Mom, for being such a bad daughter despite all your work in giving birth to me! But listen! I was only trying to save the boy in the clutches of the monster! I had no idea this would happen..."

Adelia saw Russell being tied up and thought that we were in trouble because the feline monster had taken a hostage, then she used the stealth features of her power armor to stage a surprise attack.

Though this did result in us failing to persuade Tiger Man, Adelia ended up taking the blame for shattering the sorcery stone, so we've come out ahead.

"U-um! I've heard that this country can't run without the sorcery stone, so isn't this situation pretty dire? Instead of assigning blame, shouldn't we focus on figuring out what to do about the lost sorcery stone...?"

Rose changes the subject, her conscience evidently unable to take any more of Adelie's wailing apologies.

Hearing that, Adelie raises her head as though she's found her savior.

"Th-that's right! The most important thing now is the sorcery stone! Princess Lydia, Prince Madia, you have my sincere apologies for destroying the previous stone. I will immediately send a messenger to Hiiragi and have them prepare a replacement..."

"The sorcery stone our country requires needs to match certain requirements. Can you really provide a replacement? What we need is a red sorcery stone with the highest level of mana conductivity. The only way to obtain one is to slay a superior dragon."

At Lydia's response, Adelie looks over pleadingly at us.

"Superior dragon, it seems..."

"Why are you looking at me? We're not helping you. We accepted this assignment because the request was to eliminate the feline monster and take back the sorcery stone."

"Yep, we even struggled with the lesser dragons that attacked our Hideout City. Anything bigger isn't worth the risk. You break it, you buy it."

Adelie slumps her shoulders at our cold response but perks up when she seems to remember something.

"That's right, this is Grunade. The kingdom at the foot of the Midgard Mountains! Which means there should be an ancient ruin close by!"

Lydia and the prince exchange quizzical glances at Adelie's sudden exclamation.

"Yes, there is an ancient ruin. But it's already been thoroughly excavated."

"And since it's been neglected for many years, it's now turned into a hive for monsters..."

As the two seem to be asking why anyone would want to go there, Adelie responds with a smile.

"There's a hidden door in those ruins that only we, the world's guardians, can open. A red sorcery stone of the highest quality should be stored behind it."

At Adelie's confident attitude, I can't help but ask:

"Why is there something like that stashed away there?"

I mean, I also want to know why she knows about it, but...

"That's related to the founding of this country. It's a long story, but if you want to hear..."

"Oh, never mind, then."

Adelie looks crestfallen. I guess she wanted us to hear the tale.

The prince then smirks and brightens up.

"Dame Adelheid, whom I hired, will bring us a replacement sorcery stone. That'll be the sort of achievement that puts the succession question to rest."

Hearing that, Lydia slams her hand down on the table and stands up.

"What?! She's the one who broke the sorcery stone in the first place! It's no achievement to merely make up for your own mistake! It just evens out to zero."

"That's right, it evens out to zero. Whereas you, dear sister, still have to make up for having the sorcery stone stolen in the first place!"

I glance over at Alice as the two begin the ugliest of sibling squabbles.

"Guess we'll be going, then."

"I'm sorry we couldn't fulfill your request. The results would've been different if the Hiiragi Agency of Order hadn't interfered. Hey Adelie, you owe us for our operational costs for this assignment. Here's the bill."

"What? This is a huge amount! W-wait, I don't have that kind of cash…!"

Adelie trembles at the amount on the invoice Alice places in front of her.

"Wait. We're not done yet."

Lydia stops us as we get up to leave.

"Er, there's nothing else we can do. You're not going to ask that we go hunt a dragon, are you?"

"No, of course not… But there's something else you can do, yes? For example, you could simply go and obtain the sorcery stone before she can."

Lydia smiles at us, prompting a gasp from the prince.

"Sister! Are you trying to encourage them to steal the sorcery stone from Dame Adelheid?! If the people find out you did such a thing, they will never support your reign!"

"I don't know what you're talking about. I'm just saying I don't care how they do it. So long as they bring me a sorcery stone, they'll get their payment… Besides, even if they were to take the sorcery stone by force, how would you prove it?"

Lydia lightly fiddles with her nails as she glances sidelong toward me.

"You are, in fact, a witch, sister! If that's how you want to play it, I have plans of my own!"

"There are times when royalty needs to be cunning! Look at the Grace Kingdom! They were a minor power, but now that they have a crafty, treacherous princess on the throne, they've grown by leaps and bounds. We don't need the ruler to be quite so treacherous, but the country doesn't need a king who can only offer platitudes and kindness!"

Hey, Tillis, they're having a free go at you over here.

"The young lady leading the negotiations—Alice, was it? Think carefully. It will be quite useful for you in the long run if we owe you a favor. Besides, given that you're mercenaries, reputation is everything, isn't it?"

Technically, sending out Combat Agents for hire is just a secondary occupation that allows us to obtain local currency and information about the local countries, but Alice does make a show of considering Lydia's proposal.

She's probably not pleased by the prospect of simply letting Adelie play kingmaker for the prince, and if that were to happen, Grunade's ties to Hiiragi would likely grow stronger.

"A-Agentsix? W-we technically have a cease-fire, don't we? You're not going to accept, are you?"

"Well, yeah, you're pretty strong, and it'd be kind of a hassle, so I'd rather not take it, but…"

Adelie lets out a sigh of relief at my reply.

"If you don't accept my proposal, I will tell all the neighboring kingdoms that Kisaragi is a weak mercenary company that abandons its responsibilities and runs away at the first sign of trouble. I'll do whatever I must to take the throne!"

"L-Lydia..."

Hey, Princess, your brother's totally recoiling at your machinations.

6

We put our answer on hold and return to our inn, where I lie down on the sofa to discuss our options.

"What do we do, Alice? Should we just ignore the assignment and go back to the hideout? We'll just leave Tiger Man to return to nature."

"It was supposed to be a simple job to start with, but it's starting to be not worth the effort. Still, under the circumstances, we can't afford to have rumors spread to the neighboring countries that we're a weak mercenary group. A bunch of countries and cities have offered to submit to us thanks to Lady Belial's rampage, but if we show any weakness, they're likely to all turn against us."

Oh right, there's still that problem to deal with as well.

"Plus, I don't like losing. I also don't like the idea of the Hiiragi putting on airs in this kingdom. And I hate working for free."

"For an android, you sure hate a lot of things."

I guess because of her high-level learning abilities, she's become a lot more humanlike compared to when I first met her.

"Still, as for whether to side with Princess Lydia or Prince Madia, the obvious answer is the princess. Prince Madia's too pious to work with us. In that sense, the princess would probably be more flexible."

"We've got more than our share of scheming royalty with Tillis, honestly."

...It's then that I notice there's something off about Rose.

"Are you trembling, Rose? What's wrong, did the Calorie-Z wear out?"

"No, I feel like there's a really powerful animal coming in our direction… Um, what do you mean Calorie-Z wearing out? Does the thing you give me regularly have something weird in it?"

Alice and I tilt our heads and look at Rose as she trembles on the bed, curled up under the sheets.

"Is there some sort of new giant monster approaching?"

"If that were the case, the city's residents would be in a big uproar. She never reacted like this, even when facing the Sand King. Then it must be something like the Superior Dragon mentioned earlier or—"

Before Alice can finish her sentence:

An explosion echoes from outside the inn followed by a sudden chorus of screaming.

We look out the window to see what's happened. Thugs who picked a fight with the wrong opponent sit cowering around a crater in the road.

As the city's residents start talking among one another to figure out what's going on, loud footsteps start stomping up the stairs.

The stomping stops in front of our room, and the door flies open.

"Six! Ready a bath!"

The one who orders that as the first thing out of her mouth is the long-missing Belial.

"Ready a bath? Really? Just where have you been wandering until now? It's not funny when a Supreme Leader gets lost in the wilds of an alien world."

"I was never lost. I was just working solo."

Even though she always gets lost when she gets separated from her comrades, Belial is too stubborn to admit to it.

Perhaps because of the fact that she spent most of her time outdoors, Belial's covered in dirt and dust.

"Working solo? Just what were you doing? We've had a heck of a time while you were gone. We've had all sorts of messengers coming to us to offer either friendship or submission."

"I was just hunting monsters or beating up bastards who picked a fight with me. I haven't done anything wrong. As proof, I didn't hear any announcements giving me Evil Points."

"I'm not one to talk, but please stop using Evil Points as a way to determine if what you've done is good or bad."

I don't know why she's shown up all of a sudden, but I'm grateful at least one of our problems has been solved.

Alice, who seems a bit relieved now that we've found Belial, comments:

"So we recently had two countries send us messengers of peace and five villages declare they wanted to submit to us. Just what did you do? You didn't have nearly enough manpower to actually invade them."

At Alice's critique, Belial scratches the back of her head in embarrassment.

"I would force my way into a city every time I needed to take a bath or use the restroom. Then it'd devolve into a fight whenever I threatened them to get information about Kisaragi, so I would have to smack them around, and they would just end up giving in."

"I feel sorry for those places that had to submit as an add-on to you needing to take a bath or use the restroom."

I see, she must have found out we were in this inn when she threatened the thugs outside.

"Lady Belial, you've certainly had a long, hard time of it. So shall you take a bath? Or use the restroom? Or will we go beat up Tiger Man?"

"Restroom first, then a bath… Beat up Tiger Man? What'd he do this time? …Also, Six. What's that vibrating under the sheets?"

Belial's gaze is fixed on a clump trembling violently under some sheets.

"Hey, Rose. This is one of Kisaragi's Supreme Leaders, Lady Belial. She's not an enemy, so relax already."

Rose's trembling is probably Belial's fault.

Rose peeks her head out from under the sheets but can't bring herself to meet Belial's gaze.

"My instincts as a chimera are screaming at me to stay away from her."

"Y'know, given that you spend your life like a spoiled dog, stop trying to show off your chimera-ness at times like this."

Belial's curiosity is evidently piqued by Rose, and she starts poking at the flinching lump hiding under the sheets.

"I've heard about you. You take on the powers of whatever you eat, right?"

"Y-yes… But, that only happens if I eat a lot of something."

Belial nods with a serious expression in response.

"Six, let's try feeding her an Olympic-sized pool's worth of crickets. Have Kisaragi send them to us."

"There's crickets on this planet as well, so why don't we just catch them here? I don't have that many points and don't want to spend them on crickets."

"Why does everyone from Kisaragi keep trying to feed me crickets?!" Rose wails tearfully, when I realize something.

"Lady Belial, what happened to your handheld teleporter?"

"Oh, it broke even though I didn't do anything. It was in the way, so I just tossed it."

Belial, who commented on her portable teleporter like some middle-aged boss talking about a broken laptop at work, no longer had her Kisaragi-issued portable teleporter on her wrist.

It probably broke during combat, which explained why we couldn't get in touch with her.

How was she surviving without any supplies or money or anything else?

"So what are you lot doing here anyway? Are you here to invade this country?" Belial asks curiously, as I order towels from Kisaragi.

"It's a long story, so why don't we have you take a bath first. You're giving off some serious pheromones right now, Lady Belial."

"Sh-shut up about pheromones!"

[Intermission 3]
—Naughty Memories of a Late Night with Him—

"Okay, let's move ahead a bit. How about when he had to stay at your place after he got kicked out of his apartment? Did you have any problems while living with him?"

I force my hazy mind to focus and slowly think back to that time.

He had nowhere to stay, so I let him stay in my house that night. Despite the fact that his room was far away, I remember being too nervous to sleep.

Of course, Kiku the housekeeper was there, too, so it wasn't like we were alone.

And yet I had trouble sleeping…

"…O-oh? And why did you have trouble sleeping? Did he do something to you?"

Did he do anything? Let's see… Oh, I guess maybe he did.

Yes, the day after he first stayed at my house.

That day, despite the fact that he'd been beaten to a pulp by the FlexiTeam Yoga Rangers, he said he wanted lessons on submission holds to get better at fighting…

So we ended up calling it "practicing submission holds until morning"…

"Submission holds?! You did submission holds with him until morning?! …Wait, hang on, you only 'called it' that?! What did you actually do with him?!"

…Yeah, that wasn't submission-hold training.

Well, at first I tried to teach him submission holds.

But he was so inflexible and could barely stretch, so I thought we needed to work on his flexibility first, and I started off by leaning on his back to force his legs open, then started massaging his thighs because they were so stiff from overworking them.

"Why'd you go quiet?! Just what are you remembering?!"

Stretching… Yes, we stretched until the morning…

"That's totally not stretching, is it?! Stretching is something you do to warm up! Stretching all night is something else entirely… Naughty adult stretching…!"

Oh, right. I remember being a bit stubborn about making sure I got all the knots and kinks out of his body and ended up trying to knead all of them out of him.

So instead of stretching, it was more like a full-body massage.

"C'mon, come clean already. I bet you did all sorts of naughty things, didn't you? Think back carefully. What did he say? I bet his words will tell us what you were really doing?!"

When I was all sweaty from massaging him, he turned to me and said…

"He said…Miss Yukari, you really are sexy… You're giving off all sorts of pheromones…"

"Astaroth! You need to hurry up!"

CHAPTER 4

Vote with a Clear Conscience!

1

I finally finish recounting the course of events that have brought us to using this inn room as our temporary hideout here in Grunade.

After emerging refreshed from her bath, Belial sits cross-legged on the bed, placing the sheet-wrapped Rose on her lap and cuddling the chimera like a stuffed animal.

Belial nods several times throughout the course of the tale, her features solemn, before closing it out with a final, large nod.

"I got it, I completely understand. All right, so on the matter of Tiger Man, I'll take him out myself."

"Lady Belial, are you sure you've grasped the whole situation? I mean, I think the whole thing's gotten so twisted up complex that it's hard to follow. Where did you suddenly find a new set of brains?"

I'm shocked at the fact that she's able to understand this convoluted mess of a situation.

"To put it simply, whoever obtains the sorcery stone is going to end up the king, right? I've always wanted to try my hand at being a king."

I feel a slight sense of relief when it's revealed that she doesn't get the situation in the slightest.

"Even if you obtain the sorcery stone, Lady Belial, you can't be crowned king. You don't have a claim to the throne."

While I try to persuade her with logic, Belial replies with a deathly serious expression.

"Kisaragi, people should never use the word 'can't.' Dreams won't come true if you give up on them."

"Tiger Man's dream is evidently to become an elementary school–aged kid again. Is this also something that can happen someday?"

"No, that's impossible. Tell him to give it up."

Belial completely contradicts what she said mere seconds earlier, petting Rose through the sheets. The fact that Rose is just sitting there and letting Belial play with her makes the chimera look like some sort of lap dog or something.

"All right, let's head over to those ruins tomorrow. I've already drawn up several plans, but as an evil corporation, we should employ the usual method of following the prince's party and snatching the sorcery stone out of their hands at the end."

Alice, evidently giving up on explaining the situation to Belial, begins to lay out our plan for tomorrow. Ah-ha, it's the same one we used against Heine and Russell in the ruins over in Torace.

"It's got a pretty good success rate. Since the ruins have been abandoned for so long, they've become a monster's nest. That means we can use them to clear out the monsters along the way."

"—That's our plan so far. Do you have any objections, Lady Belial?"

In a rare move for Alice, she asks for confirmation and approval from her superior, Belial. You don't see that every day. I mean, Alice usually even ignores directives from her creator.

"Sounds good to me. We've left the specifics of what to do on this planet to you guys. You just need to think of me as another Combat Agent."

Evidently, Belial's decided it's better to have only one commander for the operation and gives a relaxed smile to indicate her approval of the idea.

"Really?! I'm pretty important in this world. Can you go out and buy me some bread?"

"You go out and buy it, unless you're planning to use that bread to eat a knuckle sandwich. I want some yakisoba bread and melon bread! Don't bother coming back until you've got them."

I use my Evil Points to order baked goods that are unobtainable on this world to give to my unreasonably demanding boss as tribute. The whole exchange prompts a titter of laughter from Rose as she remains on Belial's lap.

"Boss, you and Lady Belial are real close, aren't you? You're like siblings."

"See what she's saying, Lady Belial? Can I call you 'big sister' and have you spoil me?"

"I don't want such a moronic little brother. I want one who's smarter."

Rose smiles as she continues to watch our little exchange.

Oh yeah. Before Belial had her enhancement surgery, she always used to look after me like I was her slow, delinquent little brother.

Back then, Belial's personality was the exact opposite of what it is now. She often was the one who would calm me down when I was about to charge into a group of taunting superheroes or would come to find me when I ended up getting lost in enemy territory.

When I got kicked out of my old apartment because they refused to rent to someone related to a known criminal organization, she even let me stay at her house for a bit.

When I was staying at her house, I ended up running into her at the baths pretty often, but now that I think about it, those are some nice memories.

...No, wait, thinking back on it, I'm pretty sure she kept wandering into the bath just when I was bathing.

Or actually: She would always apologize and say she didn't know I was in there, but would always make sure to get a nice, long look at my naked body.

Given how serious and well organized she was at the time, would she really have made such a simple mistake?

"Could it be that you secretly like me, Lady Belial? Do you look at me with lust-filled eyes?"

"Right now, I'm looking for the best place to punch you."

She says something that's pretty mean without so much as batting an eye, but when I think back to it, every time I'd visit Belial's room, she was usually changing. Maybe she was trying to drop hints?

"Putting aside whether you like it or not, Lady Belial, you've got a pretty dirty mind, you know?"

"All right, guess you've missed sparring with me. Step outside, dammit."

At the time, Belial was a prim and proper lady on the surface, but I know she was secretly into all sorts of naughty things.

She'd often come in to clean my messy room, but when she'd find my porn scattered haphazardly about the place, she'd pick it up and stare at it intently until I walked in.

"Why are you smirking when I'm mad at you? We're going to be doing some proper combat training. I'm not holding anything back."

Belial's playing a little coy, I guess. I can see that her cheeks are faintly flushed even as she pretends to be mad at me.

"Talking about combat training brings back memories of when I first joined Kisaragi. Back then, you drove me hard every day until I was nauseated at the end of the session."

But there's something that's changed since then.

"To prove how grateful I am for all that you've done for me, I'll show you just how strong I've become, Lady Belial."

I think back to the tough but fun memories of the past and twist my lips into a confident smile.

2

Alice is the first to greet me when I stumble out of bed a little past noon the next day.

"Hey, loser. You slept in today. We've all finished our preparations."

"Good morning, Boss loser. You said we'd be going to the ruins today, but it's almost time for lunch!"

Are these two really my partner and my subordinate?

They're being awfully cruel to someone who was beaten up just a few hours ago.

"It took a whole bunch of medical nanobots to force my body to heal in just a day! Why can't you guys be nicer to me?! Every part of me still hurts!"

Belial made sure I paid the price yesterday for going overboard when teasing her.

I took opportunities during our initial sparring to sneak in a few fondles and ended up motivating her to take things seriously.

By that, I don't mean take things seriously in an erotic sense, but to seriously put the hurt on me.

"Sorry, loser. I should've held back more. I didn't expect you to be that fragile."

"The next person who calls me loser is going to be used to harvest some Evil Points."

I try to ward off any more attempts at rubbing salt in my wounds as I check the state of my body.

It still hurts here and there, but I'm pretty functional.

"All right. Here's the plan. We'll track Adelie as she goes to recover the sorcery stone. The moment she finds it and lets down her guard, we attack her and grab the stone from her. Well, we've done it before, so the chances of failure should be pretty low."

Alice confirms the plan, prompting Rose to mumble an objection.

"This scheme really makes me feel awful when we do it. It feels like we take someone who's at the height of their sense of achievement and kick them into the depths of despair..."

While our chimera does become creepily predatory when she's hungry, ordinarily she's one of the good ones.

"If you're not too keen on it, I do have a plan B prepared as well."

"Really?! Can you describe it to us?"

Rose looks at Alice, the brains of our outfit, with eyes shimmering with admiration.

"I've got the color and shape of the shattered sorcery stone recorded, so we can send that data to Kisaragi and have a new one with the same color and shape made out of plastic or something. After that, we'll just claim that we obtained a sorcery stone and hand the replica over to them, take the reward, and bug out."

"That's even worse! Grunade needs the sorcery stone to keep functioning, so that might end up causing terrible problems after!"

Alice raises a hand reassuringly to Rose's vehement objection.

"I have a plan for that, too. We just need to have Tiger Man steal the replica before they use the sorcery stone on the artifact or whatever. Even if they send us another request to recover the sorcery stone, we just need to refuse this time."

"I'm sorry I even raised an objection, it feels like it'd be better to just grab it fair and square..."

—Deep in the woods near Grunade.

When we head to the coordinates Lydia has given us, we see what look like ruins.

It's a facility that's smaller in scale than the one in Torace, and it's made of a material that's similar to concrete.

Alice stares at the ruins from a distance before taking a look around the area.

"There's signs of an encampment near the ruins, so it seems like they've already started their search. So I'm guessing the secret door that only Adelie can open is probably already open, yeah? Let's just have Lady Belial roast everything in the ruins."

"My turn, huh? One ruin roast coming right up."

"After which Adelie will somehow make it out of the ruins and the intense heat ends up melting the sorcery stone, right? I can already see how that plays out, so please stay back, Lady Belial."

Belial slumps her shoulders as she's told to stay put, prompting Rose to nervously try to reassure her.

"…Hey. Adelie's emerging from the ruins. And she's got some company we don't want her to have."

I guess because it took a while for me to wake up, Adelie has already finished her dive into the ruins and is emerging with her party in tow.

"It looks like a film crew or something is mixed in with the knights. Does this planet have TV?" Belial asks, evidently impressed, but that's probably the bad company Alice is referring to.

Trailing behind Adelie and surrounded by knights belonging to the prince's faction is a man carrying something that looks like a television camera.

"Yep. Despite the fact they still use outhouses, they have these weird TVs powered by some mystery sauce. I guess it's all part of this planet's whole magic schtick."

"Oh, right, I saw that in the reports… Wait. That means if we grab the sorcery stone, it'll all be broadcast to the populace, right?"

When Lydia asked the prince yesterday:

"Besides, even if they were to take the sorcery stone by force, how would you prove it?"

The prince said, "I have plans of my own." I guess this is what he meant.

"The problem is with the fact that they already have the sorcery stone. If not, we could just have Lady Belial incinerate them before they can film it… Maybe we can hit the camera from a distance? Though even if we take out the camera, we can't be sure they don't have any other filming equipment. In that case, should we just hit the cameraman…?"

"No, Miss Alice, we can't do that! Even during a war, the postman, the cameraman, and the beetle merchant are off limits!"

I get the postman and the cameraman, but why do the laws of war protect the beetle merchants?

Just then:

Belial, who has been keeping watch over our surroundings, spots something.

"…Mm? Hey, isn't that Tiger Man? What's he doing over there?"

When we follow her gaze, we find Tiger Man lurking in some bushes.

"Good catch, Lady Belial. Tiger Man's tough to find when he's hiding in foliage. He's probably trying to snatch the sorcery stone from Adelie. He's been on a sorcery stone–collecting kick lately."

"You can't become king if you're not a royal, even if you have the sorcery stone, right? What's he planning to do with it?"

Belial tilts her head and watches Tiger Man slowly approach the target.

"There's someone on this planet who can manipulate time. Tiger Man believes that if he can get a powerful-enough sorcery stone, she can eventually make him a child again, so he's been trying to find every powerful sorcery stone he can get his hands on."

"Maybe it's because I'm kind of stupid, but I don't understand what Tiger Man's trying to do."

Well, I don't get it, either.

…Just then, Tiger Man makes his move.

He probably sees that Adelie and her party are tired from dealing with the monsters in the ruins.

"Ah, Tiger Man's about to spring into action. I've never seen him look so committed."

As Belial notes, the usually laid-back mutant has a look of intense determination on his face.

"Oh, there he goes! Boss, are you sure we should just be sitting here watching?" Rose asks with a note of concern, perhaps because she's fond of him.

"Yeah, just watching is kind of dull... Lady Belial, shall we make a bet on whether or not he succeeds in nabbing the stone? I'll bet some information on one of Lady Lilith's screw-ups on him succeeding."

"Then I'll bet a compromising photo of Astaroth on him failing."

"You shouldn't gamble like that! And that's not what I meant..."

"Yo, looks like Tiger Man's taken the initiative. But the camera's got a good view of him."

As Alice notes, the camera's captured the entire progression of Tiger Man's sneak attack.

Tiger Man lets loose with a jump kick against Adelie, as though to pay her back for the other day.

Adelie somehow manages to block his kick, but the impact tosses her back.

The knights around her intervene and help cushion the blow as she's thrown toward the ruin wall.

Meanwhile, the cameraman manages to capture the whole exchange without missing a single beat.

"That cameraman is more agile than Tiger Man or Adelie."

"That's cuz film crews are sent to get footage of monsters in the Cursed Woods. There was a lot of buzz around the recent dragon documentary where they managed to get shots of a dragon's lair and the dragonlings inside."

I really want to watch that documentary, and I'd love to poach him for our team.

"Adelie's working with the knights to fight back, but Tiger Man's still got the advantage."

Alice provides commentary, watching the exchange like a neutral observer.

Whatever else he might be, Tiger Man's still one of the most powerful of our mutants. Even with knights in support, he's still going to be too much for someone like Adelie, who's about on my level.

Shield-carrying knights in full armor are tossed aside like tin soldiers, and before long, Adelie is cornered on her own.

The image of a humanoid monster cornering Adelie against a wall looks pretty dodgy from an ethics point of view, so the cameraman makes sure to capture the situation from multiple angles.

"Lady Belial, looking forward to seeing that compromising photo of Lady Astaroth."

"It's not over yet. Pay close attention, Six. I'll show you what it means to work smarter, not harder."

Belial then jumps out of the tree cover we'd taken shelter behind.

She makes the most of her enhancement surgery–boosted physical abilities and dashes forward at a speed that a normal person would struggle to follow by sight.

Belial quickly closes in on Tiger Man as he faces off against the knights.

"<Been a while, Tiger Man. Glad to see you looking well! Hang on, I'll execute you in a sec!>"

"<What are you doing here, Lady Belial?! I can think of lots of reasons why I should be put to death, but neow's a bit sudden if you're not even going to hear mreee out!>"

Tiger Man quickly leaps backward to dodge the smiling Supreme Leader's punch.

"Hey, Alice, what are we going to do? She's so dead set on winning her bet with me that she's charged out without thinking."

"Even I haven't planned for this. She's shouting at Tiger Man in Japanese, so it's only a matter of time before people find out he's affiliated with us. Don't worry, I've made preparations to bug out."

As I'm trying to figure out what to do about Belial's sudden burst of unexpected activity, Adelie, who's ended up being rescued by Belial, faintly blushes as she looks at Belial's back.

I guess from Adelie's point of view, Belial looks like a hero suddenly intervening to save her in the nick of time.

The cameraman rolls along the ground to get the best angle on the flame-haired beauty's sudden arrival.

"<Then I'll give you ten seconds. Try to convince me.>"

"<When I snuck in to steal the sorcery stone, Princess Nadia was sitting there by herself looking lonely. When I asked her what was wrong, she spoke to me without any fear and told me she was sad because she wasn't able to do anything to stop her older siblings from fighting.>"

...Oh?

"<When she saw me carrying the sorcery stone, she didn't try to stop me, and instead encouraged me to take it, because it was causing the fight between her brother and sister. And then she said that if she were to vanish, maybe her big brother and big sister would put aside their differences to find her, so she asked me to take her with me in exchange for me taking the sorcery stone... When a kid asks something like that of you, you can't just turn her down, can you?>"

...Tiger Man's so serious that he's forgetting to add his usual meows and purrs when speaking.

As Alice translates Tiger Man's Japanese for Rose, I feel shame at having rushed to judge him.

"Boss, Miss Alice! I don't know what Tiger Man is planning to do, but we should go, too!"

Rose, deeply moved as Alice tells her what Tiger Man said, clenches her hand into a fist and holds it up.

I reach back and unholster my pistol to support Tiger Man.

"<So I made a decision. I'll smack the idiots neglecting their little sister and fighting over the crown. Then, I'll obtain a new sorcery stone and take that with Princess Nadia to—>"

"<You've said enough, Tiger Man!>"

Belial interrupts his passionate monologue.

Belial looks upon Tiger Man with a serious expression, as though to say he doesn't need to speak any more.

Then after giving a nod of understanding—

"<I said you had ten seconds! Your story's way too long, and it didn't convince me, so I'm going to execute you!>"

"<That's way troo unfair! Meow!>"

—I have no time to intervene before Belial attacks.

3

Adelie bows her head along with the cameraman and knights.

"Thank you very much! Without your help, he would've taken the sorcery stone!"

Under assault from Belial, Tiger Man started yowling as he dodged her attacks, then tossed a stun grenade before retreating.

As a woodlands combat expert who specializes in sneak attacks, Tiger Man's fond of making use of stun grenades.

It's why he even wears sunglasses that protect against the flashes.

"What I didn't expect was…"

Adelie looks over at us with a torn expression.

"That this gentlewoman is Agentsix's superior. Lady Belial, yes? Allow me to once again express my gratitude. Thank you so very much for helping me."

Adelie eyed us warily when we emerged from the copse of trees, but now she's let down her guard.

"I wanted to finish him off myself, but, well, I'm glad to see you lot are unharmed."

Pleased that Belial is worried about her, Adelie blushes faintly.

"Do you have a history with that monster, Lady Belial?"

"Yeah, he used to be my underling."

...

"Lady Belial, what are you saying?! They didn't know Tiger Man was one of ours!"

Adelie freezes up in shock, and Belial just smirks at my urgent whispering.

"If you're going to make it as part of an evil corporation, you need to know how to always live on the razor's edge. Screw playing it safe. You and I are both villains; live for a good time, not a long time!"

Why does the Kisaragi Corporation always seem to attract these sorts of people? I wish they'd pick up some common sense from me.

I mean, this is Belial we're talking about. If things go wrong, she's probably figuring she can brute-force her way out of it.

"You just enjoy riling everyone up, don't you, Lady Belial? Just recently, we were in similar circumstances where we had to try to make sure we didn't tip off the other party. Combat Agent Ten started enjoying himself by trying to make us break character and mess up like you're doing right now, Lady Belial..."

"She's just using a bit of Kisaragi-brand humor. Of course, we don't know anything about that monster."

"O-oh, I see now! Heh, you had me going there for a minute! I even heard you talking in a language that sounded like the one the monster was using..."

Belial does a complete 180, probably because she doesn't want to be mentioned in the same breath as Ten. Adelie looks at Belial with eyes shimmering with admiration and holds out her hand.

"Lady Belial, your sense of justice is remarkable! I'm Adelie the Gray Savior, Apostle of the Hiiragi Agency of Order!"

"So you're an enemy!"

Adelie, who was holding her hand out for a handshake, instead gets a headbutt from Belial and crumples to her knees.

"Who else did you think she was? You told me yesterday that you completely understood the situation after I explained it to you."

"I was just letting you talk for maybe eighty percent of it, duh. Still, this makes things a lot easier."

Belial smiles maliciously as she grabs Adelie by the collar and lifts her up.

"Adelwhatever of our competition. You admit that we saved you despite the fact that you're our competitor, right? And you admit that if I hadn't stepped in, you would've lost the sorcery stone, right?"

"O-of course… We, the Hiiragi Agency of Order, are a just and righteous organization. We repay our debts."

While Adelie's got tears welling in her eyes from the pain of the headbutt, she doesn't give an inch even as Belial has her dangling off the ground.

"So long as you understand. Then let's make this quick. You're going to repay us with that sorcery stone."

"What?! What are you talking about?! I can't possibly do that! Technically, it isn't mine to give…!"

While the knights around Adelie ready their weapons, the most they can do is look on at Belial from a distance as they recall how easily she defeated Tiger Man.

Adelie, hanging off the ground as Belial holds her aloft with one hand, tucks the sorcery stone against her stomach to show she won't give it up.

"I-I'll repay the debt with something else! I can't give this to you; there's people who need it!"

"…Fine. Then I'll accept something else."

Evidently impressed by Adelie's defiance, Belial sighs and sets Adelie on the ground.

Adelie looks up at Belial with a sigh of relief.

"Your organization's name, Hiiragi. It's too close to Kisaragi, and it's confusing to people. Change your name to make it clear you're on the other side. Use one of those normal names like Whateverangers."

"What the heck!"

As Adelie cradles the sorcery stone and backs away on the ground, Belial snaps at her.

"No on the sorcery stone, no on the renaming! You're being awfully unreasonable considering you're in my debt!"

"I-I am not! Hey, people watching this broadcast, am I being unreasonable?!"

The cornered Adelie makes her appeal to the camera, when Alice murmurs something to Belial.

"...Fine. We'll just say you owe us a favor for this one. Hurry up and take your sorcery stone to the people who need it."

Adelie cowers as Belial suddenly becomes calmer, but she screws up the courage to announce to us.

"I'll be sure to repay this debt! But I win this time! The Hiiragi Agency of Order..."

Adelie pauses a moment to build up dramatic tension.

"Will never bow to evil!"

And makes a pose toward the camera.

"..."

"W-w-wait! Are you mad because I was mugging for the camera?! I'll apologize for that, but we'll be on our way for now!"

Belial, irked by Adelie's posing, wordlessly shuffles toward her, prompting Adelie and her knights to flee.

Having returned to our inn, we turn on the mystery TV.

And here they return in triumph! Dame Adelheid, the Apostle summoned by Prince Madia by the Hiiragi Agency of Order, has brought back a sorcery stone! The crisis that was feared when the national treasure was stolen has now been averted!

On the screen in front of us, Adelie is waving her hand to the camera, and the reporter declares loudly that it's all thanks to Prince Madia.

I look at this less-than-pleasing segment and turn to Alice as she dangles her legs off the side of the bed.

"Hey, are you sure we made the right call here? It looks like game, set, match to me."

"As I told Lady Belial at the time, there's still a plan C to go. But to get that to succeed, we can't have her going on a rampage on camera."

Rose, who has been strangely quiet, says in response with a downturned gaze:

"Um…is there any way we can help Tiger Man this time? He seems to have been really dedicated to helping Princess Nadia, and I have to admit I'd like to help make her wish come true, too."

It all got lost in the hubbub because Belial cut him off, but I'm pretty sure Tiger Man wants to get Nadia on the throne to stop this stupid fight over the succession.

I don't know what she's like since we haven't met her yet, but based on Tiger Man's story, she seems better than the other two.

"I can't say anything about that for now. Tiger Man's started it on his own, so it's his responsibility to get it done."

Rose seems to deflate even more at Alice's harsh judgment.

"But Tiger Man is Kisaragi's most powerful mutant. Even without our help, he might be able to snag a sorcery stone or two on his own."

"Miss Alice…you're right. Evidently you can obtain one of those stones by defeating a superior dragon, and I can see Tiger Man going and hunting one!"

Something about Rose's statement makes something rattle around in my memory.

Yeah, I feel like we're forgetting something concerning sorcery stones…

As I'm trying to remember whatever that might be, Belial excitedly asks Alice:

"So what are we going to do now? You have this plan C, right?"

"The plan itself is pretty simple. But to do it, we need a sorcery stone."

Alice then hops off the bed.

"The sorcery stone should arrive in this city soon. Let's go pick it up before Tiger Man notices!"

We leave the city of Grunade and walk down the highway leading to the Midgard Mountains.

...How long have we been walking?

The sky starts to get darker, and we start setting up camp. Just then...

"Hey, there's someone coming this way."

With her exceptionally good instincts, Belial notices there's someone approaching us from the other end of the highway.

I turn to face that direction at her prompting.

"You there! Could we trouble you for something to eat?! I am Snow, Knight Commander of the Grace Kingdom Royal Guard! Do not worry! I have no hostile intentions, and I have money to offer! So please...please give her something to eat!"

Snow is there, with a slumped Heine on one shoulder, using her sword as a cane.

4

"Hey, gimme another piece of that bread! Also, more water!"

"I'll take more bread, too! Ah... The last time a simple piece of bread tasted this good...was when I was given a piece of rye bread at a soup kitchen after going five days without food when I lived in the slums...!"

It seems they were famished; the two start vacuuming up the food I ordered with my Evil Points.

As Snow weeps while gnawing on a piece of bread, Heine also starts to tear up for some reason.

"You've had such a hard life… Here, have my piece of bread, too."

"Don't be ridiculous, Heine, you need to eat that. I haven't forgotten that you lied, telling me you didn't like the gaminess of monster liver, and gave it to me, even though you love it so much, you were salivating just looking at it! I'm going to feed you until you burst!"

They exchange tearful words as they eat their bread. Is it just me, or are they weirdly close now?

I guess they became friends during the course of their survival training.

"Here, this meat's ready. It's times like this I'm glad I'm a fire mage. It makes it easier to control the cooking fire."

"Heh… That's the Heine I know. I'll gratefully take it. But you take this skewer that looks the tastiest."

As they laugh and offer each other barbecued meat skewers…

"If you two don't want them, I'll take them."

""Ack!""

Completely oblivious to the friendly mood, Rose gobbles down the two skewers.

"Why are you eating that skewer! I was trying to give it to Snow to eat…"

"Heine was close to death earlier! Heine should have been the one to eat that…"

Heine and Snow exchange glances after yelling at Rose and blush.

"You two look ready to start a shipping company. When'd you start dating?"

"You moron! Don't tarnish our friendship!"

"You always have your mind in the gutter! What can't you just

appreciate a friendship forged in the fires of adversity that goes beyond race and country?!"

Pretty sure they're just delirious from exhaustion. I bet things'll go back to normal in a few days.

"Well, I'd forgotten all about you two ever since we teleported you away. What were you up to these last few days?"

At my casual question, the two look at me, eyes wide with fury, and tremble in anger.

"What do you mean what were we doing?! As you can see, we were fighting for our lives! The dragons chased us down and took our rations, then the rest of our equipment…!"

"We needed to keep a fire lit through the night, and there's a limit to how much magic I could use. Snow would hunt the predators that attacked us, and I'd use my magic to cook them… We made it through by relying on each other!"

Guess Alice was wrong about greater dragons being too smart to want to attack humans.

I exchange glances with Alice about that, and she simply shrugs it off as a miscalculation.

Belial, who'd been quietly wolfing down meat, looks over at the pair curiously.

"So why did you teleport them out there? Was it some sort of prank or punishment?"

"Why are you making it sound like you're uninvolved? We sent out search parties every time there was a high-energy surge to find you when you were lost, Lady Belial."

Well, toward the end, we did start to enjoy it and started picking points on a whim…

Belial gets shifty-eyed for a moment then finishes her skewer.

"I wafn't loft…"

"Are you still saying that? If you stay in denial, we'll just leave you here."

Rose, evidently satisfied after eating more skewers than anyone, smiles over at Snow and Heine.

"Anyway, I'm glad you two are all right. Russell and I were also tied up and brought here to Grunade against our will."

"You've been through a lot, too, it seems… Which reminds me, I've been wondering, who is the lady there?"

Snow points to the pouting Belial.

"Oh, right. I hadn't introduced you yet. This is Lady Belial, one of the Supreme Leaders of the Kisaragi Corporation."

"I see… A pleasure to make your acquaintance, Lady Belial. I am Snow, Kisaragi Combat Agent, and Knight Commander of the Grace Kingdom's Royal Guard. I hope to be of use to you…"

Showing off her refinement as a knight commander, Snow curtsies elegantly.

At receiving Snow's introduction, Belial then claps her hands together as though she recalled something.

"I remember your name. I saw it in Six's report! You love money and magic swords, and you kissed Six when he couldn't move!"

"Ack! What are you doing?! Stop! Quit struggling!"

I restrain Snow when she attacks me at Belial's statement. Alice, having finished cleaning up the camp, states to the group:

"All right, then it's time to head back to town. The original plan was to spend the night here then start looking for Snow and Heine, but they found us first. It's better to get back to the inn and sleep rather than camp out here, isn't it?"

"Yeah. You guys came out to look for us? If you're nice enough to do that, maybe you could have not teleported us to the middle of nowhere in the first place…?"

"I agree… Well, we were all right in the end. Survival training isn't too bad, and it did give me a chance to get to know Heine."

Heine smiles a bit shyly at Snow's words.

"It's true that we came to find you, but technically we weren't looking for you two. We were looking for Heine's sorcery stone."

"What?"

It seems they've become synched over the past few days; Snow and Heine both tilt their heads quizzically.

"Oh, I remember now! The sorcery stone Miss Heine has was the one Tiger Man obtained by fighting and defeating a dragon!"

Rose claps her hands together as though everything clicked for her, prompting Heine to glance down at the sorcery stone on the outside of her hand.

"Meaning you need my power now?" Heine says with a confident smirk, prompting Alice to interject.

"What we need is the stone. It needs to be a red one that's come from a dragon."

...Heine tearfully resists as she holds the sorcery stone to her stomach to keep us from taking it.

"This stone is precious to Heine. If you intend to take it by force, I don't care who you are, I'll help her fight to keep it," Snow declares loudly, then draws her sword and steps in front of Heine like a knight protecting the weak.

Heine, who was curled up and crying over her stone, looks up at Snow as though she were a shining knight, wiping the tears from her face and rising to her feet.

She stands behind Snow, dropping into a stance to offer magical support.

"I know full well I can't beat you all, but even then that's..."

"If we take the sorcery stone to the princess, we'll get a huge payout. I'll give you a big bonus, too."

Snow's pure expression of chivalric virtue wavers at Alice's statement.

"What it...means to be a knight...but..."

"Lady Belial's the most powerful warrior in Kisaragi. Careful you don't die resisting her."

At my words, Snow then quietly lowers her gaze.

"...S-Snow? We're BFFs, right? You're not going to abandon me, right?" Heine says worriedly to Snow, whose shoulders are trembling.

"...If I recall, that sorcery stone was a present from Tiger Man, right? Then, if you hand it over and get a bonus, you'll come out ahead, Heine."

"What the hell are you talking about?! The day we split that last piece of dried meat, you said I was the first demon friend you ever had!"

......

"Under these circumstances, it's useless to resist! Then it's smarter to hand over the sorcery stone and get our share! You got that sorcery stone for free; don't be greedy!"

"You bitch, that's the worst kind of betrayal! That's why I hate humans! Thinking back on it, it's because of your greed that I had to try to curry favor as much as I did with that prince in Torace! You really need to stop being so fixated on money!"

I figured things would go back to normal within three days, but they didn't even last a day.

The two glare at each other and close the distance between them, each looking for an opening.

"Blast you, cursed demon! Now that I think about it, I haven't liked you since the moment I first saw you!"

"That's my line, dammit! Don't mess with a former elite of the Demon Lord's Army!"

As the two women begin grappling and brawling, Belial looks at them with an exasperated sigh.

"Hey, Six, you should pick your subordinates more carefully."

"Lady Lilith told me the exact same thing."

5

The day after, the pair's friendship shattered like glass, and Belial had to silence their squabbling with force.

Having grabbed the sorcery stone, Alice and I are going to the receiving room in the castle to meet with Lydia.

"What do you want now? I'm so disappointed in you lot. My chances of taking the throne look quite grim."

Thanks to the fact that the prince went out and loudly proclaimed his acquisition of a sorcery stone, there's an almost funeral-like atmosphere among Lydia's supporters.

As the princess lets out a heavy sigh, Alice places the sorcery stone in front of her.

"...This is a sorcery stone of the highest quality... And it's red—does that mean you slew a dragon?!"

"How we acquired it is a company secret. While our delivery is late, it's too early to give up on the throne."

Lydia shakes her head despite Alice's confident statement.

"...Even if I have a sorcery stone, it's far too late now. The election to determine the next ruler is going to be held soon. My younger brother, who acquired a stone first, is being feted like a hero. It'd be impossible to make up for that gap in popularity unless my brother makes a serious mistake... This despite the fact that I need to do everything in my power to get the throne..."

Alice looks over at me ,and I produce a single book.

The cover says *Election Manual for Evil Corporations* in this country's language, but the original had been written in Japanese.

Lydia's unable to take her eyes off the book's title, and I use this opportunity to land a follow-up blow.

"This is a vote-gathering manual that our organization developed.

It's a very popular book with politicians, and we have a money-back guarantee if you don't see results."

"Look at the wraparound band on the book. Princess Tillis of the Grace Kingdom gives her approval of it. If you buy the book now, it comes with a free sorcery stone as a gift."

As Alice and I give our sales pitch, Lydia picks up the volume and clasps it to her chest.

She looks at us expectantly, and we give our final pitch.

"You can get all of this with the originally promised payment!"

"And as a limited-time service to you, Princess Lydia, we'll provide our expert assistance in putting the manual's methods into practice!"

"Please, let me buy this book!"

Deeply moved, Lydia immediately decides to purchase the manual.

[Crown Election in Ten Days]

Having converted our inn room into an election office without anyone's permission, we immediately get to work.

The innkeeper looks a bit troubled by our activity, but Alice has given him a large amount of money, so hopefully he'll let it slide for the duration of the election.

Lydia's subordinates will also be doing some electioneering, but we have our own separate election office.

"Have you all memorized the contents of the manual? Even if it comes to trial, I'll serve as your lawyer and make sure you get off. I've got bail money, and I promise you high pay during the election! So go out and get electioneering!"

"This is right up my ally. Leave it to me!" Snow responds enthusiastically to Alice's announcement.

"I-I was also an officer in the Demon Lord's Army. I'll do whatever it takes to seize victory!"

Heine clenches her fist tightly, eager to compete with Snow.

"...Boss, can I just go back to Hideout City?"

"Who's going to play the straight man if you leave? I'll give you some Calorie-Z later, so tough it out."

The level of motivation in the room is a little uneven.

Belial glances around the office with a sentimental look, as though it's bringing back some memories.

[Crown Election in Eight Days]

And in more royal news: It's only been a few days since Prince Madia was all over the headlines for acquiring a sorcery stone, but the good news continues. Princess Lydia has just announced that she has acquired a sorcery stone that's of even higher quality than the one recently obtained by Prince Madia. At this announcement, Prince Madia has issued a statement that his earlier acquisition of a sorcery stone makes him the worthier candidate for the throne. Meanwhile, experts await Princess Lydia's response—

The news plays from the mystery TV embedded in our office wall.

For the moment, Alice is handling everything to do with the TV station.

Those who win over the press win over the people.

Still, grassroots actions are also important.

I put on a mask to completely cover my face and head out to the nighttime streets of the city.

[Crown Election in Seven Days]

The night is growing late, and the crowds in the gathering places around the city are starting to clear out.

"Hey buddy, on your way home from the bar? I wanted to ask ya something. Who are you planning to vote for? Prince Madia or Princess Lydia?"

"Eep! A-ahm…I'm planning to vote for Prince Madia."

I nod intently when the young man on the way home from the tavern answers my question.

"I'm glad to hear that! If you said you were going to vote for Princess Lydia, you would've been in a lot of trouble! Y'know, folks like me would be in a lot of trouble if Princess Lydia took the throne. It'd make business real hard for us!"

"I-I see…"

<Evil Points Acquired>

I lightly press my fist against the confused man's chest.

"You tell your buddies that they need to vote for Prince Madia. That they should avoid voting for the princess even if their lives depend on it. Got it?"

"…I…I under…stand."

<Evil Points Acquired>

I confirm that the young man nods before walking away.

I'm sure the others are busy with electioneering right now as well.

I head back out into the streets to look for my next target.

[Crown Election in Six Days]

And now, more election news. In a recent press conference, Princess Lydia issued a plea: "It's wrong for siblings to fight over the throne. If we have money to spend on that sort of effort, it should be spent on the people instead. If my brother will promise to rule justly, I'm willing to withdraw my candidacy." Her statement is strongly at odds with Prince Madia's insistence that he alone is worthy to rule—

Since my work mostly takes place at night, I wait in the office until nightfall.

As I'm listening to the news, a busy-looking Alice remarks:

"Things are going well so far. Snow's been caught by the authorities, but if she doesn't get greedy, she should be out on bail pretty quickly."

…….

"Meaning, Snow's out for the election, then."

"Exactly."

Snow did some good work.

I should take a page from her book and try harder.

[Crown Election in Five Days]

"Snow's maintaining her silence. That alone is enough to be a big blow to the other side. We've also leaked information to the TV station we paid off. I'm looking forward to the news tomorrow."

"The more days she stays silent, the more she gets paid, right? If we're not careful, she might not speak even after the election's done and end up staying in jail forever, no?"

As I'm worrying about Snow, the office door suddenly swings open.

Rose hurriedly rushes into the office, out of breath.

"B-Boss, I got news! Miss Heine's been arrested by the police!"

"Woo-hoo!"

"Good job, Heine!"

Rose casts a skeptical look at us as we let out a cheer.

First Snow, and now Heine. I should put some more effort into this myself.

In other election news: There have been a growing number of incidents of voters being threatened with harm if they don't vote for Prince Madia. Due to the seriousness of the allegations, the authorities have attempted to question Prince Madia and his advisors, but he has refused to allow their investigations, claiming, "This is a trap set by Lydia's party. We have done nothing wrong."

[Crown Election in Four Days]

Next in election news: Concerning the white-haired woman believed to be a supporter of Prince Madia, despite the fact that there have been multiple testimonies from voters that she offered them money to vote for Prince Madia, the woman continues to maintain her silence. Prince Madia has issued the following statement: "There are no white-haired women in our party. I've never met this woman, so she must be part of Lydia's party." Currently the issue continues to ripple through the electorate. In a related incident, a demon woman has been arrested for making similar offers—

"Agentsix! I know you're in there, Agentsix! Aren't you ashamed for using such underhanded tactics?! If you don't open the door, I'll kick it down!"

I hear shouting from outside the office door.

Waiting in front of the door, I check the position of the camera before sending Rose out as a messenger from the rear entrance.

"It'll be about five minutes until the police get here. I'm hoping you get some good shots, ace."

The cameraman, the one who accompanied Adelie, gives a thumbs-up and nods at Alice's remark.

He's a freelance cameraman, and Alice spent a huge amount of money to hire him.

"If you're not going to come out, then I'll carry out justice in the name of the people! Taste justice!"

I tense my body and prepare myself for a strong blow.

"Gray Thunder!"

"Guh!"

My arms are hit with a powerful impact as the door is kicked down and I'm thrown back.

"Six! Are you all right?! You're badly wounded! Hold on!"

"Guh… Alice, I'm sorry… Looks like I'm done for… Don't let those evil bastards supporting Madia win…"

"?!???!?!???!?!"

Adelie, having kicked down the door, goes into a complete confused panic as Alice and I play out our little drama.

And the camera has captured the property destruction and assault.

"W-w-w-wait! Stop! Don't film this! I didn't do this on purpose! It's an accident…"

Adelie desperately tries to defend herself from the shocking footage captured on tape, but the cameraman, caught in the moment of grabbing a huge scoop, pays no heed to her words.

Just then:

"Mr. Policeman, over here!"

"Hey, what are you doing?! ...Ah! Another one of Madia's people!"

"?!"

Realizing she's been had, Adelie lets out a scream of frustration as the police conveniently enter the room.

"Agentsiiiiiiiiix!!"

[Crown Election in...]

In election-related news... The recently arrested suspect, Adelheid of no known address and self-proclaimed Apostle, has confessed to being affiliated with Prince Madia. According to sources within the authorities, the accused has an extensive criminal history in the Grace Kingdom, where she was arrested multiple times for causing general unrest...

We listen to the news as we wait for the long-anticipated election results to be announced.

"The latest poll conducted the day before voting day had Princess Lydia with seventy-two percent support, Prince Madia with eleven percent, and the rest of the field with seventeen percent."

The tension eases in the office as the results of the poll are announced.

"Barring a hell of a last-minute surprise, we should be fine. But things went better than expected this time. Usually, we'd have to call in Lady Belial after this..."

Our interference operations into our opponent's electioneering had gone better than expected, so there was no need for Belial or me to get involved.

The original plan was for me to disguise myself as one of the prince's campaign operatives and go about threatening the local residents before having Belial drive me off.

Then we were going to advertise that one of Lydia's allies had defeated an operative who was trying to coerce the residents into voting for the prince.

"You don't need to be concerned about how I'm feeling. Besides, watching the election interference and harassment brought back some nice memories. You remember back when the superheroes tried to get involved with politics and we did everything we could at Kisaragi to stop them?"

"Oh yeah, I remember that. The best part was when Lady Lilith, buoyed by our success, got it into her head to run for election herself and ended up dead last."

See, in Japan, a candidate running for office has to pay an election deposit.

Now, those who obtain a certain number of votes get that deposit back, but Lilith failed to hit that threshold and went into a crying fit when the government refused to refund her the deposit.

"But wait, didn't that happen before you got your enhancement surgery? I thought you had no memories from before it happened, but I guess sometimes they can just come bubbling up."

Belial offers a small smile at my comment and softly shrugs.

The Prince's chances are pretty much finished. It's pretty clear who's going to win this election.

Certain of victory, we wait calmly for the results…

…Only for Princess Nadia to win the crown somehow.

[Intermission 4]
—Precious Memories of Him and My Friends—

"Sorry, I didn't mean to lose my cool like that. Then, let's move ahead a bit in terms of time… Hmm, should we even continue this treatment? I have a feeling it might end up being a lot more trouble than it's worth…," Lilith says, then falls into a troubled silence. But it'd be a bit of a problem for me if we stop the treatment right here.

I feel like I'm on the verge of remembering something really important.

"Oh well. Whatever problems might happen will come later. We may as well go as far as we can. I'll add a little more of the drug now."

Maybe we should stop the treatment here…

"Hey, there's no need to be so worried. You know just how intelligent I am, right?"

It's because I know your intelligence so well that I'm starting to feel a bit anxious…

"Oh? It seems you're starting to regain memories of when Yukari had dropped any filters when speaking to me. Okay, then let's try remembering things that you enjoyed. Times and events that are precious to you. For example, I'm sure there's plenty of things involving us," Lilith says as though anticipating a specific response from me.

Things that I enjoyed… Let's see, a little after he joined Kisaragi, he stopped holding back, and he started clashing with Astaroth every time they laid eyes on each other.

I was always the one who'd step in to try to mediate their dispute, but Lilith would never fail to find some fuel to throw on the fire and escalate the argument.

Kisaragi was still a small company, and every day was one challenge after another, but those days were also a lot of fun.

Oh, I remember something about Lilith, too. Let's see…

"Yes?"

Election… When we'd grown to a midsize corporation, the superheroes who saw us as a threat tried to enter into national politics.

They were trying to tie us up with legislation and lawfully sap our power…

"Oh, yeah, I remember that. You felt some reluctance to follow my proposals and took quite a bit to commit to your part. That sentimental part of you is a lot like him."

That's right. Because he's a bit of a coward at heart, he couldn't bring himself to commit big acts of villainy, and he often came to me for advice.

"Just because you lost your memories doesn't mean your past crimes never happened. Now, think back and remember. What do you see?"

Lilith looks at me with expectant eyes, and I simply tell her the first image that comes to mind.

"I can't forget you bawling her eyes out when she lost her entire election deposit."

"You don't have to remember that!"

FINAL CHAPTER

Being the Boss They Can Depend On...

1

In the woods near Grunade.

Having finishing putting up the tent, I sit down by the campfire and say to Alice:

"I've suspected it for a while, but I'm pretty sure Tiger Man is an idiot."

"You think the people in Kisaragi are anything but morons? I don't count, I'm an android."

Then I don't count because I'm an enhanced human.

Besides, it's going too far to say everyone's an idiot. There's still our last hope, Astaroth…

"Lady Astaroth's the queen of the idiots, considering she's the one who came up with the idea of forming an evil organization to take over the world. As for the second-biggest idiot, I nominate Lady Lilith."

"Stop it, don't anticipate what I'm trying to say. I'm pretty sure our Lady Lilith is number one by a pretty big margin."

As Alice and I banter…

"This isn't the time for this! How are we going to fix the gigantic mess we're in now?!"

The candidate no one was expecting to win, Princess Nadia, the youngest of the three princelings, has ended up with the crown.

As for how it ended up this way, well, it's because all of our misdeeds were revealed to the public.

Namely, the fact that Tiger Man, the monster guilty of stealing the sorcery stone, is affiliated with us.

Tiger Man himself revealed that we were behind everything, from trying to frame Hiiragi for the theft by having the letter sent to Grunade, to the various underhanded tactics we used to ruin our opponent's reputations in the election.

As for why he did that—

"Honestly, I underestimated Tiger Man. I figured he was just a pervert who liked to meow and purr while admiring the lolis. I had no idea he'd be willing to risk everything, even his own life, for the sake of saving a little girl."

"That miscalculation is on me. I didn't expect Tiger Man to go that far. While gigantification is the ace in the hole for mutants to use to take superheroes with them when all else fails, it's a last resort that costs the mutant years of lifespan. And not only did Tiger Man do that, he then went and turned himself in to make the princess win the crown. Honestly, I underestimated him. Tiger Man's the lolicon's lolicon. A real credit to his kind."

To make Nadia queen, Tiger Man used the mutant's trump card of gigantification to take a sorcery stone from a greater dragon living in the Midgard Mountains.

He then gave Nadia the sorcery stone before turning himself in to the authorities, revealing that he was part of our organization.

Thanks to his bombshell revelation, Lydia, who had pulled us into the election, lost almost all of her support, while the prince just couldn't stage enough of a comeback to boost his flagging poll numbers, and so…

"I didn't expect Russell to throw his support behind Princess Nadia, either. That pretty much settled the race."

Russell is protecting Nadia from any threats at the moment.

He must have been influenced by Tiger Man's dedication. Russell had enthusiastically campaigned for Nadia.

The image of a beautiful young maid helping the young princess was a hit with the populace.

What sealed the deal was when Adelie, one of the prince's supporters, publicly outed Russell as a boy.

For some reason, that resulted in a massive surge of support from female voters and ended up settling the race in Nadia's favor.

This was despite the fact that Russell's technically part of Kisaragi, too…

"Well, it's a star-studded cast, a young child princess with a cross-dressing handsome boy maid. To the people, the monarch is as much decoration as anything else. They want someone that looks good. After all, most of their lives won't change much no matter who's in charge."

"I-I'd like to think things are a little better in Grace. I mean, people say a lot of things about Princess Tillis, but she's popular with her citizens…"

At Alice's cynical, world-weary observation, Rose can only mumble a less than confident defense.

"Still, what the hell are Tiger Man and Russell thinking? Even with Princess Nadia making a case for him, it's only a matter of time before he's executed. Yes, he turned himself in, but what he did isn't easily forgiven or forgotten."

"I mean, Tiger Man's earned his fate, but with Snow and Heine still in jail, we can't just leave…"

"Come on, Boss, let's at least try to help Tiger Man, too..."

The situation is so bad that even Alice seems at a loss for what to do.

That, and there's a reason we're camping out here.

Rose detects something and turns her eyes toward the brush.

There's some rustling from the other side, and appearing from between the bushes...

"Caught some wild Evil Points! Hey, Six, hurry and convert them to points! There's quite a few others lurking around, but I brought all the ones I could carry."

"Can we stop calling prisoners 'points,' please? Even I'm a little weirded out by that."

I don't know which faction they belong to, but Belial returns to camp carrying four of our pursuers.

Usually, being chased by an entire country should be a pretty perilous situation, but to Belial, it's just an opportunity to farm some Evil Points by capturing soldiers from both factions.

As for converting them to points... How am I supposed to do that? Torture these soldiers wrapped in steel wire?

Alice suddenly bows her head to Belial.

"Lady Belial, I'm sorry for bringing you all the way from Earth only to end up in this mess. The way all of this has played out is my fault."

"M-Miss Alice?"

Rose can't help but be taken aback at Alice's unusually meek and apologetic attitude.

"I didn't expect things to go this thoroughly pear-shaped. I should take responsibility and go self-destruct in the middle of Grunade."

"Hey, don't even think about it! I told you that self-destructing is out of limits!"

I grab Alice by the collar to stop her, prompting a small chuckle from Belial.

"Alice, you overthink things because you're so smart. Just take a simpler look at things."

Belial smiles as she gently musses Alice's hair.

Alice looks up at Belial through the mussing. It's pretty clear Belial doesn't have a good grasp of the situation.

"...You say that, Lady Belial, but the situation is thoroughly fubar. I have no idea what Tiger Man and Russell are thinking, while I'm sure Snow and Heine, who were in jail, have been taken hostage. The prince and princess are sure to put their differences aside for now. Thanks to Tiger Man's betrayal, Kisaragi has to deal with the Hiiragi Agency of Order and Grunade, while they've got hostages to use as bargaining..."

Belial holds up a hand to stop Alice mid-sentence.

She then nods as though she understands everything perfectly.

"So what? We just need to beam them all down at once."

......

"Hey, Six, help me with persuading Lady Belial. This Gordian knot of a situation is going to take a while to explain."

I look between the confidently smiling Belial and Alice with her troubled expression and come to a realization.

"Lady Belial's right. We've been worrying too much about the little kinks in the rope."

"...Six?"

Alice evidently thought I would try to stop Belial and looks up at me with a quizzical expression.

"As Lady Belial says, we're overthinking this. Why did we even try to hide Tiger Man's crimes? It's because it was too early to go to war with this country. Why were we trying to avoid fighting the Hiiragi Agency of Order? Because it was too early to have a proper scrap with them."

At that, Alice falls silent, lapsing into thought as Belial continues to tussle her hair.

"...You mean with Lady Belial here, we can deal with the two countries combined on equal footing? …True. What does it matter if Tiger Man confessed to being a member of Kisaragi? So what if they know we were behind all the election shenanigans? We're an evil corporation! We don't bother untying knots; we just cut through them! If they wanna complain, we'll just face them straight on!"

"Yep, all we have to do is go on the diplomatic offensive with Lady Belial as our backup. The agents we sent out got those cities where Lady Belial went on a rampage to submit by threatening them, right? Then, it's time for some gunboat diplomacy! That's what you were trying to say, right, Lady Belial?"

There's a reason she's a Supreme Leader; she can take this tangled mess of a situation and…!

"Nope! Wrong!"

I can't contain a surge of irritation as Belial laughs in response to my question.

"You're still overthinking it. Kisaragi is an evil corporation bent on world domination. And there's only one thing we do against our enemies."

As we stay silent, Belial playfully smiles and declares:

"Invade!"

2

Just as people are rubbing the sleep out of their eyes and waking up all around the city of Grunade, a giant explosion echoes through the air.

They jump out of their houses and begin raising a fuss as they look around in a panic.

"W-what is it?! Are dragons attacking?!"

"This city is protected by the Midgard Mountains. There's no way dragons would attack!"

"But there was evidently an explosion in front of the inn the other day."

"I heard that it was a red-haired woman using magic..."

The residents speculate among themselves, only to freeze when they hear the follow-up announcement.

"Good morning, people of Grunade! We are the Kisaragi Corporation! We have a message for the Grunade Royal Family! Come to the clock tower in the next five seconds! If you don't comply, we will burn down a building for every second you don't show!"

"What are you doing?! They can't possibly make it within five seconds!"

I grab the loudspeaker from Belial to keep her from making any more ridiculous demands.

We're standing at the very top of the clock tower in the middle of the city.

Having infiltrated town, we're now making unreasonable demands to the Grunade Royal Family.

"Oh, calm down. This is a negotiating tactic Lilith taught me. You put up unreasonable demands first, then you put out the demands you actually want, which will seem more reasonable in contrast."

"I see. You've put some thought behind it. I'm sorry to doubt you."

I've heard that when doing business, it's a pretty common tactic to start with a sky-high price and make the buyer think you're giving them a deal by giving them the price you actually want later on.

Belial then takes the loudspeaker back and makes her next announcement.

"All right, five seconds was a bit unreasonable! We'll give you a small concession! You have ten seconds to—"

I snatch the loudspeaker from Belial again, when there's a commotion at the bottom of the clock tower.

Alice and I peer downward.

"Lady Belial, one of the royals showed up. They did it within the ten seconds you asked for."

"See? Unlike Lilith, my demands are reasonable."

I'm pretty sure there are times when she's more demanding than Lilith, but I decide it's best to keep my silence.

Lydia's standing there with a large group of soldiers at the base of the tower. I guess she was planning to lead them in an effort to find us this morning.

"Hey, Six. There's a woman with resting bitch face glaring at me…"

"That's Princess Lydia, the elder daughter of the king and the oldest of the royals. I think her glaring at you is understandable. You did just wake up her country at this unreasonable hour and start threatening them."

Of course, she threatened to spread bad reviews about us, so I think we're kind of even on that front.

Belial nods, processing my words before taking the loudspeaker from me, then shouts down to the base of the tower.

"So you're that stupid bitch Lydia! I'm going to smack you, so come up here! If not, I'll reduce your city to a burnt-out wasteland!"

"Y-you disrespectful commoner! You show up out of nowhere and start this nonsense?! Who do you think you're talking to, you self-important peasant…"

I give Rose the signal even as Lydia begins to bicker with Belial.

"Ahm… Just to double-check, are you sure you want to do this, Boss? I feel like we'll be crossing a point of no return if we do this…"

"We've already blown way past that line. Besides, remember what Lady Belial said? They're wild Evil Points waiting to be harvested!"

Rose drags the four prisoners we captured in the woods to the top of the tower.

"My family has a long, distinguished history! Certainly more

than some princess from a backwater nation like this! Keep talking, and I'll actually give you something to whine about!"

"How dare you insult our country?! You'll pay for that! You lot! Break down the clock tower door!"

We ignore the rapidly escalating argument between the two women and force the tied-up prisoners to walk to the windows.

Lydia, who has been wailing insults at Belial, freezes when she sees the faces of the prisoners.

"Do they look familiar to you? If they do, we'll trade them for the prisoners you've got. If they don't, they're useless to us, so we'll just throw them away!"

<Evil Points Acquired>

"She's a true Supreme Leader, all right. She's a damned sight more impressive than Lady Lilith."

"Hey, Alice. I'm getting Evil Points just following orders. Are you sure we should've left the planning to Lady Belial?"

Lydia's gone deathly pale, speechless at the sight of the prisoners. She hurriedly raises her hands to plead her case to us.

"Y-you wouldn't really do that in the middle of the city, would you? Let's negotiate. Yes, two of them are my followers, but—"

Before Lydia can finish, Belial grabs one of the prisoners by the scruff of the neck and dangles him over the side.

"The only thing I wanted to know is if they looked familiar to you! I'm giving you thirty minutes. Hurry up and bring out our underlings!"

<Evil Points Acquired>

"I-I accept! We'll do a prisoner exchange, so stop dangling him over the side!"

Lydia hurriedly issues orders to her soldiers. She might have a bit of a scheming side, but she's a sheltered princess in the end.

"That princess has a lot to learn. I'm sure part of it is the fact that the people are watching, but she's started negotiating with terrorists.

If it were Tillis, she'd probably manage to produce a tear or two before insisting sadly that royals won't negotiate with terrorists and leave them to their fate."

"H-Her Highness probably isn't that ruthless! Maybe!"

"If you really believe that, at least avoid saying 'probably.'"

Lydia then glares up at us after sending one of her soldiers off to the castle.

"There, are you satisfied? If that's good enough, then release your prisoners… Also, allow me to point out that of those four, only two of them are my followers. The one you're dangling isn't one of them. But as a princess of this kingdom…"

"Then I guess we don't need him."

<Evil Points Acquired>

"Nooooo!"

Belial lets go of the prisoner before Lydia can finish her statement.

The bound and gagged captive falls with tears streaming from their eyes.

As Lydia screams, Belial tosses the loudspeaker aside and grabs my knife from my hip.

She leans out the window and winds up—

"Noooooo…ooh… Oh?!…"

She throws the knife with laser-like accuracy, not even leaving a scratch on the prisoner as it pins them by the collar to the stone face of the clock tower.

The prisoner is pinned to the wall of the tower right before hitting the ground, and they pass out while foaming at the mouth from terror. Lydia's legs give out from under her as she slumps to the ground.

The soldiers continue to exude hostility toward us, but they look taken aback and faintly cowed by Belial's display of godlike skill. She casually picks up the loudspeaker.

"Which ones are your followers? I'll release the other captive who isn't your underling!"

"Just release them normally! Don't drop them! They might not be my follower, but they're still one of my precious subjects! Also, please let me finish!"

3

The prisoner exchange ends up being arranged to occur outside the city.

Having been thoroughly thrown for a loop by Belial, I guess Lydia wanted to avoid any further negotiations inside the city. The spot they specified is a barren piece of terrain with a cliff at the back.

It's a nice, empty piece of land, and unless someone bothers to scale the cliff, there's no chance of being ambushed.

"Things are going smoothly thanks to Lady Belial. We should be able to recover Miss Snow and Miss Heine without any trouble," Rose says with a note of admiration as she leads the prisoners by a length of wire.

Belial's actions earlier are probably what you'd consider the very model of a Kisaragi employee, but…

"You know, you're starting to be more accepting of outright villainy lately. What happened to the pure and conscientious Rose that I first met? At least try to avoid ending up like one of the Kisaragi Supreme Leaders, okay?"

Belial, who has been cheerful thanks to Rose's praise, pouts in response.

"You're the ones who asked me to negotiate. I was just doing what you asked. I was fine with just forcing our way into the castle."

"I'm pretty sure you and Lady Lilith are the only ones who'd call that negotiating."

"Boss, your negotiations aren't that different. I mean, do you remember how you tried talking it out with Tiger Man the other day?"

Just as we're placidly waiting outside the city, Lydia appears at the meeting spot with a large contingent of soldiers in tow, her expression clearly communicating her displeasure.

The soldier at the very back of the group leads Heine, who looks relieved, and Snow, who's making no effort to conceal her irritation, by a rope.

Lydia clears her throat to begin the prisoner exchange when—

"Alice—!"

—Snow suddenly shouts, silencing everyone there.

Having built up a friendship with Heine, it seem Snow has remembered what it means to be a knight. I'm sure she's going to tell us not to worry about her.

"I've kept my silence until the very end! And I tried to resist them from taking me out of jail! Don't forget that you promised to reward me for as long as I stayed silent!"

"...Yep. Good job. I'm proud of you. I'll add a little extra to your payment."

Alice smiles softly after momentarily freezing at Snow's obsessive fixation on payment, even under these circumstances.

...You know, she's still one of my subordinates.

"Hey, Six, I mentioned this before, but you really should pick your subordinates better."

"I don't think you're one to talk, being the Supreme Leader of a group of nothing but eccentrics and misfits like Kisaragi."

Lydia gapes at the exchange, before she begins to tremble.

"H-how strong is your need to insult me...?! Do you understand the situation? I've heard the rumors of how powerful Kisaragi's mercenaries are; that's why I hired you in the first place."

As Lydia's anger builds, I remove the shackles from our prisoners' legs, and when I lightly push them in the back, they run off without bothering to look back at me.

At the same time, Snow and Heine have their restraints removed, and they start to make their way through the soldiers in our direction.

"But the real reason I hired you is because our countries' soldiers lack experience fighting monsters... Grunade is a holy country where the protection of the Midgard Mountains keeps all monsters but dragons from its lands. We're not used to fighting monsters, but we've got plenty of skill when it comes to fighting people! Now that we have our hostages back..."

"Hey."

Belial interrupts Lydia's threatening remarks with a single word.

"Now that we have our hostages, there's no need to hold back. You better be ready for what's coming."

"That's my line! ...For the love of the gods, let me finish!"

The moment Lydia angrily shouts out the words, the ground under the soldiers behind her erupts upward like an exploding volcano.

The surrounding land bursts upward and the soldiers, thrown high into the air, scream, before raining down to the ground with a hail of pebbles.

Since they're normal humans, Belial must have held back quite a bit.

I don't think any of them have mortal wounds, but it still looks like a scene from hell with the shattered ground, the soldiers lying in their heaps, and Snow and Heine getting caught in the explosion.

As the groans of soldiers spill into the air, Lydia, who ducked and covered her ears at the explosion, tentatively turns to look.

"Ahhhhhh! M-m-my followers... My soldiers!"

<Evil Points Acquired>

It was a small explosion by Belial's standards, not even requiring her to make any gestures before unleashing it.

Lydia wails at the sheer, brutal violence that neutralizes her soldiers in a single breath.

I wish they wouldn't give me Evil Points for this. I mean, I'm only

here as one of Belial's accomplices; these points make it seem like I'm one of the main villains.

...Seeing Lydia's face take on a look of complete despair, Belial nods approvingly.

"Lydia of the Grunade Kingdom, was it? I'm going to give you a good, hard smack now."

"Why?!"

Belial lands a follow-up blow, even as Lydia reels from having all of her soldiers taken out in a single blow.

Oh, right, I told Belial about the fact that Lydia basically tried to blackmail us.

Belial hates it when people disrespect Kisaragi, so I guess she wants to exact a price for that.

Alice and Rose go to recover the pair of prisoners who got caught in the blast, as Belial cracks her knuckles, approaching Lydia, who remains cowed on the ground.

Just as things seem to be at their worst for Grunade, I hear a familiar voice ring through the air.

"That's enough!"

The person who appears at the top of the cliff like a hero saving the day is—

"Diiiiiie!"

"Aaaaaaaaaaaaaaaaack!"

—Adelie, who tumbles from the cliff before she can identify herself, losing her footing when Belial destroys the ledge she's standing on with a jump kick.

Belial is, of course, ridiculous for shattering a solid-stone cliff face with a mere kick, but Adelie's also pretty ridiculous given that she stands up and dusts herself off like nothing happened after falling from that height.

Adelie herself probably wasn't expecting to suddenly be attacked before she could say anything.

I mean, both she and Lydia at least deserve to finish their lines.

Despite not taking much in the way of physical damage, Adelie still seems to be recovering mentally as she looks around blankly before pointing her finger at me.

"I-I…I don't know why I get treated like this, given I'm the victim this time, but anyway… That's enough, evildoers!"

Adelie stands there ignoring Alice as she drags the pair of unconscious prisoners along the ground, waiting for our reaction.

"That was pretty unfair, Lady Belial! You've completely thrown her for a loop. Remember that we're not supposed to attack superheroes when they're showing off after their arrival, transforming, or in an emotionally moving situation."

"Well, Adelie's not technically a superhero, so it's not a violation of Kisaragi's rules of engagement. But she sure does time her appearances like a superhero, which makes me want to attack her."

"Please, at least listen to me!"

Adelie somehow gathers her wits and glares at us.

"Agentsix, look what you've done! You've got a heck of a lot to answer for! But first, say you're sorry! Sorry for trying to frame me for that tiger beastman's crimes! Also, while interfering is part of all elections, I think you guys went too far!"

I exchange glances with Belial as Adelie shouts at me.

I'm pretty impressed that she's got the guts to lecture us in this situation, but does she really understand what's about to happen to her?

"I know that look you're giving me! It's the pitying look you give to an idiot! Even I'm not so reckless as to face you guys alone," Adelie says with a triumphant look, but it doesn't really fit someone who fell off a cliff before she could get off her heroic pose.

"The prince is already on the way with his troops after hearing your broadcast earlier. I just came early to slow you down until they can arrive!"

Belial and I exchange glances again at Adelie's comment.

True to Adelie's statement, Prince Madia arrives with his troops in tow a little while later.

The moment he sees us, the prince's blood pressure appears to spike, and a vein pops on his forehead as he shouts at us.

"Thanks to your meddling, our kingdom's facing a terrible crisis! First, you will hand over my followers! Then, we'll crush the mercenaries of Kisaragi with the help of Hiiragi!"

He doesn't have as many soldiers as Lydia, but it's still a pretty big group.

However...

"...Hm? W-what's going on here...?"

It seems he's finally noticed the mess around him, realizing that the lumps buried under the gravel are soldiers. A look of troubled confusion spreads across the prince's features.

"M-Madia..."

At first he struggles to recognize the tremulous voice addressing him, but then he furrows his brow as he realizes who's addressing him.

"L-Lydia?! How did this happen?! Aren't your personal soldiers on par with the royal army...?"

The prince is clearly taken aback when he sees Lydia slumped on the ground, tears welling in her eyes and the fight sapped from her expression.

"Excuse me, Your Highness. Do you mind looking over this way for a moment?"

When I call over to him, Adelie, who's been tied up with steel wire and lying on the ground at my feet, pipes up.

"I-I'll never bow down to evil! Your Highness, please do as your conscience says you must!"

"Y-you villain… You utter bastard…! You weren't satisfied with just tearing down my sister, but you've also reduced Dame Adelheid to such a pitiable state…!"

Seeing his sister and Adelie in their current state, Madia incorrectly assumes that this is all my fault. The prince's voice trembles with rage and his cheeks flush with anger as he yells over at me.

Wait, I thought he and Lydia didn't like each other.

"…Fine. We'll allow you to return to your lands. In exchange, you will not lay a finger on Dame Adelheid."

The prince seems to be under the impression we've taken Adelie as a hostage, but he's mistaken.

Having already recovered Snow and Heine, we don't actually have any need for further hostages.

"No, we've only tied her up because she said she was here to keep us busy."

"Yep, she's been causing a racket. We'd be real grateful if you'd take her off our hands."

The prince looks a bit confused at our words.

"Just what are you lot after? You ally with my sister, only to turn around thoroughly to break her will to resist; you take my followers as hostages, but then say you'll return Dame Adelheid to us. Honestly, I can't even begin to comprehend what your goals are."

"Well, it's not like we're doing this because we want to. This whole to-do is a result of our mutant, Tiger Man, going off half-cocked on his own, so…"

"Yep. We've both had a lot happen, but a good chunk of it's just because we weren't reading from the same script, never mind being on the same page. With the Demon Lord Realm gone, you guys are our neighbors now. It might take a while, but why don't we work on finding an arrangement that works for all of us?"

At Alice's proposal, we hear the sound of something hitting the ground echoing from nearby.

We turn to face the source of the sound to find Lydia, who's somewhat recovered her wits, throwing her fan down against the ground.

"I can't let things end as they are! That's because I need to become queen! We definitely can't let my little sister Nadia take the crown! And...I can't let Madia do it, either!"

"L-Lydia...?"

At her sudden change, everyone stares at Lydia in slack-jawed amazement, before the princess, having gotten everyone's attention, continues.

"Do you know how our kingdom came to be? ...No, I suppose none of you have any way of knowing. What the sorcery stone is used for, or what happens as a result!"

There's a desperate intensity to Lydia's exhausted features.

As everyone falls silent at her intensity, the princess begins to explain in a tone of abject despair:

"Once, this land was overflowing with monsters. That was because this country had water in greater abundance than others... And in that world, the people were forced to choose. To live in lands that had ample water, but were swarming with monsters, or lands with relatively few monsters, but which were harsh, arid wastelands. Both choices were death sentences in their own right. But the artifacts from the distant past made it possible to survive..."

<Evil Points Acquired>

Just as Princess Lydia gets to that part, and everyone is caught up in listening to her story...

I hear the Evil Point acquisition announcement go off, and the ground suddenly bursts upward, throwing everyone into the air other than the Kisaragi personnel. As dirt and screams rain down once more, Belial says without the slightest hint of remorse:

"I'm tired of all these convoluted stories! Summarize, dammit! Summarize!"

"I've been thinking this for a while now, but Lady Belial, you really need to work on your patience."

4

We leave Snow and Heine with Rose and head to Grunade castle.

For some reason, Adelie's tagging along with us.

As for everyone else, both the royals and the soldiers look like they'll be out for a while.

Rose called over for some officials as she was carrying Snow and Heine back to town, so we decide to just leave the soldiers to them.

Adelie's probably not going to try anything. Belial's already showed her how futile it would be to resist…

"Hey, Agentsix, what are you planning to do by breaking into the castle? If you're planning something evil, I can't just stand by and let it happen…"

"We're going to make the person who caused all of this unpleasantness—the tiger beastman you're familiar with—take responsibility for what's happened. I mean, in the end, it's all his fault."

Belial confidently leads our procession, neutralizing the soldiers who notice us and turn their weapons on us without the slightest hesitation.

Adelie watches as the soldiers attack, only to be taken down one by one, and says to me in a trembling voice:

"…H-hey, Agentsix. I feel like I'm witnessing some terrible villainy."

"You're no bystander, either. We've come too far to just let you walk off."

"You came uninvited; the least you can do is stay. If Tiger Man resists, you're pitching in."

Adelie, knowing Tiger Man's strength, doesn't look pleased at that prospect, but it seems her innate sense of righteousness wins out in the end, as she follows us without complaint.

Princess Nadia is probably on the very top floor.

For whatever reason, the rule seems to be that kings and heroes just seem to like being in high places.

Just as we're about to reach the top floor, Belial, who's been leading us, stops.

When I look, there's a single man standing in front of a giant, ornately decorated pair of doors that appear to lead to the throne room.

"You're in the way. Move."

The man pays no heed to Belial's command.

There's an aura about him, as his body easily carries the weight of full-plate armor, and his stance exudes confidence.

I doubt he could beat Belial, but he's probably one of the stronger individuals on this planet.

"He's at least as skilled as Snow in terms of swordsmanship. And he's got the strength and endurance to easily move around in heavy armor."

"Oh? He must be pretty good to be rated so highly by you. This might be entertaining."

Adelie nods in agreement after Alice and my exchange.

"He's this kingdom's greatest knight, and a true warrior that even I treat with caution. I'm sure you've all at least heard his name. His name is—"

The man doesn't even have a chance to speak as Belial punches him without a word, sending him flying.

He slams into the wall and lies there unmoving. Alice glances down at him as we walk past.

"Tell me the name of the man even you treat with caution, eh?"

"Your partner rated him highly, too! He fought me to a standstill when we sparred! H-hey, keep up, Miss Belial's going to leave us behind!"

Adelie says this in a rush before Belial opens the doors!

"Mr. Tiger, say *ahh*."

"Hey, my mouth's not wherrre you should ssstore prrrrudding. Make sure Rurrsssell gets srrrome, too."

In a room where a lavishly decorated throne sits atop a luxuriantly rich carpet, Tiger Man is lying on the floor with his head in Russell's lap, being offered a spoonful of pudding by a little girl.

"...Well, I don't dislike pudding. But I can eat it myself."

With that, Russell holds his hand out to the girl, freezing as he turns his gaze toward us.

Tiger Man, noticing Russell suddenly go rigid, follows Russell's gaze and freezes himself when he sees us.

The little girl, seeing Tiger Man, Russell, and our group all staringly blankly at one another, shyly looks up at us.

"Hello..."

"Well hi there, miss. We have business with Mr. Tiger, so can you follow this nice lady and play with her for a bit?"

"Huh? M-me?! Ahm, errm, okay! Heroes are also friends of children! I'll teach you my ample repertoire of cool poses!"

Adelie panics for a moment when we push the child onto her, but she seems to catch on and accepts.

Based on how close she is with Tiger Man, I'm guessing this little girl is Princess Nadia.

As Adelie takes her by the hand, she looks back multiple times toward Tiger Man before leaving the room.

After making sure the door has closed behind them, Belial lets out a slow breath.

"Now..."

"I have one concern about dying. May I ask a favor of you?" Tiger Man, sitting respectfully, says without purring or meowing.

Belial nods as though offering a final bit of compassion to the mutant, who seems to have made his peace with his own death.

"All right. Say it."

"If I die, Nadia will be exposed to danger. Could you please place her under your protection?"

As Tiger Man tries to protect the young loli princess even in the face of imminent death, Russell raises his voice in a panic.

"W-wait, what the heck?! Hey, Tiger Man, what do you mean you're going to die?!"

Belial tilts her head quizzically at Russell, who she's meeting for the first time.

"This is your first time meeting him, isn't it, Lady Belial? This is Russell, whose hobby is cross-dressing."

"Oh, the one who showed Lilith his dick. I don't have anything to say about anyone's hobbies, but don't try to show me your junk, okay?"

"Well, that's a terrible first impression you've given her! It's not MY hobby to cross-dress, and I didn't want her to see it! …H-huh? I-I can't stop trembling."

Russell, like Rose, seems to instinctively fear Belial, and he begins to tremble.

Belial suddenly raises her voice as Russell tries to hold his ground and stand in front of Tiger Man to plead his case.

"Making excuses is beneath you! Why would you dress up like that if you didn't like it?! I have no interest in shaming anyone for their kinks, so be proud of who you are and what you like!"

"N-no…! It really isn't my…"

Belial hikes up Russell's skirt, even as he insists on arguing.

"You can't wear shorts like this under your skirt and claim that it's not something you enjoy. Don't live in denial. It's fine. It looks good on you, and you look cute. Be more confident in yourself."

"She isn't listening to me at all…"

Even as Belial pats his head, Russell grips the hem of his skirt tightly, eyes welling with tears of frustration.

Tiger Man then raises his face.

"Lady Belial, you just said you won't shame anyeowone for their kinks."

"...I didn't say that."

The pervert who had forced a cross-dressing chimera to offer his lap to him as a headrest, then had a little girl feed him pudding, seems to have found the faintest glimmer of hope shining at the end of the tunnel.

The sicko mutant jumps to his feet and points his finger at Belial, shouting angrily.

"It's nyeot frair for a Kisaragi Supreme Leader to go brrack on their worrrd! Lolicons are people, too! Making a little girl feed me a little pudding is hardly something I deserve a death sentence for!"

"You idiot! You kidnapped a child! I sent you out here as the ace in the hole to back up the Combat Agents because you're the most powerful of the mutants, yet somehow you've caused the most problems!"

Russell trembles, cowing as the two begin to fight, and looks over at us pleadingly.

He probably wants us to intervene, but there's no way a rank-and-file Combat Agent can step in and stop a fight between the most powerful Supreme Leader and the most powerful mutant.

Tiger Man, who seems to have given up any pretense of contrition, then pulls Russell over to him and sticks his tongue out tauntingly at Belial.

"Besides, Lady Belial went and hiked up Rurrrssell's skirt, too! I'll send a report to Kisaragi telling them that you peeked at a boy mrrraid's panties!"

...

"You know that evidence can be destroyed, right? When did you delude yourself into thinking you can beat me?"

"I'm nrrrrot thinking I can win. But I can at least send some reports to Kisaragi befrrrore you can kill mreee! Mrrr!"

As the two of them face off, looking for an opening, I hear a large number of people approaching the room.

"There's people coming. Maybe go for a temporary cease-fire?"

"Mrralready knyeow that. Frrrrom the sounds, there's mrraybe ten to fifteen and they're all arrrmmmed."

"There's fourteen. One of them isn't carrying a weapon. That Lydia girl is bringing her soldiers here."

……

"You can't even tell that much? Dummy! Moron!"

"You're a Supreme Leader, but you can brrre such a brrrrat!"

These two fighters, perhaps because their titles have "the ultimate" or "most powerful" in them, can sometimes be a lot of work to handle.

"And why the hell did you do something this stupid in the first place?! You knew sex crimes against children result in a death sentence!"

"I tried to explain on that front, but you wouldn't even try to listen to me! Also, I swear on anything holy and unholy that I haven't actually done anything to her! Meow!"

"They're about to enter the room! Can't you two get along right now?!"

As I yell at the two of them, the room door is thrown open.

Just as Belial predicted, it's a party of soldiers led by Lydia.

Lydia, having taken a quick look around the room, then raises her voice.

"Where's Nadia?! I swear I won't hurt her, so tell me where she is!"

"And then what, mrr? You'll just demrrand that she give you the throoone!"

Lydia glares at Tiger Man's comment.

"Yes, of course! I need to take the throne, not Nadia, not Madia! Even if I take the throne, my brother will become king soon after, so you stay out of it!"

Lydia's desperate plea seems to have tipped Alice off to the fact that not everything was as it seemed.

"What do you mean your brother will become king soon after? What are you planning to do with the throne?"

Lydia swallows a breath at Alice's calm question, containing her emotions and turning to her soldiers.

"...Leave the room. I need to explain things to these people."

Lydia orders the soldiers to exit the chamber even as they object to leaving her alone with potential hostiles. Once the room is empty except for members of Kisaragi and herself, Lydia says with a thoroughly exhausted expression:

"I need you to finally, actually, listen to how the Grunade Kingdom was established."

She smiles a wistfully sad smile as she speaks in a soft, scratchy voice.

5

After hearing Lydia's explanation, Alice says:

"So this kingdom has used an artifact generation after generation to protect it from monsters, but it needs sorcery stones as fuel. A single stone can only run the artifact for a hundred years. It's almost time to replace the stone, but only the ruler can switch out the stone. So Princess Lydia was throwing a tantrum because she wanted to replace the stone herself."

"I mean, when summarized, that's what it boils down to, but the way you phrased it makes me sound kind of stupid. Can't you make it a little more..."

Alice summarizes Lydia's ten-minute story in less than twenty seconds.

"If you want to be the one to swap the stone so much, then you should just say that. Then at least your brother might listen to you."

I say this wondering why she couldn't have done such a simple thing, to which Lydia smiles sadly.

"The artifact is one of those mixed blessings where the person who swaps the sorcery stone usually ends up dead. That's why, typically, an old king will do the exchange as his final duty to his kingdom."

"Killing you for switching batteries? That sounds like the mother of all lemons. Is it just leaking out current?"

"N-nn, I already explained the reason for it earlier in quite a bit of detail..."

......Wait.

"So basically, you want to take the throne because you don't want your brother or sister to die, and you intend to swap the stone and die for them?"

"I thought I'd been saying that the whole time..."

At that, all of the Kisaragi personnel in the room smirk.

"Aha, so you're a *tsundere*, eh? Well, hate to break it to you, but the *tsundere* boom's over."

"I have no clue what it is you're talking about, but I understand that you're mocking me!"

Still, if that's the case, it changes the calculus.

"So what'll it be, Tiger Man? Do you really want to keep Nyowdia on the throne?"

"Of course nyeot! If you wanna replace the stone, then I'm leaving that up to you, Llllydia."

He really is harsh to everyone but lolis.

It's then that Belial notices the throne at the far end of the throne room.

Her eyes shine like a kid in a candy store's, and she heads over to the throne, practically skipping on the way.

She had given up quickly on understanding Lydia's explanation, and, I suppose in an effort to listen to it later to get the gist of it, had placed a digital voice recorder down to record the explanation.

Belial sits without hesitation in the chair that only the country's ruler is supposed to sit in.

"W-wait! Where do you think you're sitting?!"

Lydia looks shocked and confused as Belial engages in an act of lèse-majesté that would have resulted in instant execution were there a living king.

Sometimes even I'm taken aback the things she gets up to.

"Lady Belial, you can't sit there. That's a spot for really important people to sit."

"I'm a really important person in Kisaragi, aren't I? If you don't like it, then you can try to force me to get up."

Well, yeah, she had mentioned wanting to become the queen, but this is maybe taking this whole acting-on-a-whim thing too far.

"Tiger Man, can I get your help? I'll take the right, and you can approach from the left."

"Mrrrkay. Lady Belial, you're being farrrr too irresponsible given the circumstances. Mrrrm."

As we approach to drag her off the throne, Belial sits regally upon the throne and issues her edicts.

"You there, the rank-and-file lackey with an uppity face. If you don't offer us tribute of a pork bao within three seconds, you'll be executed."

"You really can be a menace… C'mon, Lady Belial, we'll be in a lot of trouble if one of those uptight soldiers sees you like this."

"Big women are awwwfurrrl. Yep, lolis are better, mrrrm!"

Having started her little playacting as queen, she points her finger at Tiger Man.

"The beast that made a risqué statement. You creep us out and thus are sentenced to death."

"Oh yeah? Well, with Six by mrrry side, we can put up a decent frrright!"

As Belial does as she pleases, even Alice looks a bit exasperated.

"Hey, you sure about that, Lady Belial? I can't just let it go."

"Oh, c'mon, tell her, Alice. If I'm being honest, I wanna sit on that chair, too. You can't be the only one to get your way, Lady Belial."

"Meowlice, use your logic to shoot down Lady Belial's arguments until she breaks down crying!"

Yet, for some reason, Alice also looks exasperated with us as we try to egg her on.

"Lady Belial isn't playing around. She's saying she's going to take the throne and do the sorcery stone swap herself. I can't allow our irreplaceable Supreme Leader, who we're borrowing from HQ, to do something that dangerous."

"What?"

Everyone present lets out an exclamation of surprise at Alice's statement.

"...Didn't Lady Belial just sound surprised, too?"

"Nope... W-well, yeah, I was surprised. Y-y-know, because Alice understood what I was trying to do."

Oh, that's the face she makes when things go in an unexpected direction and she doesn't know how to deal with it.

I suppose I have no choice, I'll step in and...

"Lady Belial, are you sure about this? You're large, unreasonable, and a troublesome boss, but we can't let you do this."

"Th-that's right. I don't know you very well, Lady Belial, but you're one of the most important people in Kisaragi, right? Something this dangerous should just be left to this country's people."

Tiger Man and Russell follow up with statements of concern over Belial's safety before I can say anything, but these are the sorts of words that are really effective, given how dedicated she is to taking responsibility.

Lydia, who has been quiet up to this point, forces a sad smile to her lips.

"This is a responsibility for a member of the royal family to bear. I very much appreciate your sentiment, and I thank you for the kind offer, but that's all it can be. I do have one thing to ask of you instead… Please keep the truth of all of this from my brother and sister."

She says the words most likely to hit Belial right between the eyes.

6

—The Midgard Mountains.

The artifact at the heart of all this trouble lies hidden within this mountain range that stretches for several miles near the Grunade Kingdom.

"Nyope nyope nyope! Nyoooo way, that's definitely impossible!"

"Stop mewling, Tiger Man! A Kisaragi mutant has no business saying the word 'impossible'!"

Having approached the Midgard Mountains, we listen to a detailed explanation of what we're there to do, because, well, we can't very well be horsing around with our lives on the line.

"Tch, so it's not to do with exchanging the stone killing you at all! If that wasn't the case, you could've mentioned it earlier!"

"N-no, I tried multiple times to explain… N-never mind."

Lydia slumps, emotionally drained from her explanation, while Belial looks as lively and enthusiastic as ever.

Tiger Man, who was meowing noisily just now, then says in a perfectly sober and serious voice:

"I think we should just give up on this country and make one of the older kids the king. Mrrr."

"Will this beast only be tamed by my sister? I think I look pretty similar to her."

Lydia pouts at Tiger Man's statement.

"Mrr. Yeah, you do look alike. Bruuut, I don't have any interest in old meo-aids."

"W-who are you calling an old maid, you disrespectful cur?! I'm only nineteen! Now try saying that again!"

"Mrr. Yeah, you do look alike. Bruuut, I don't have any interest in old meo-aids."

Lydia punches Tiger Man's stomach several times after the mutant frankly repeats his previous line word for word. Alice, who had been using some sort of measuring device to investigate something, declares:

"There's no doubting it now. The princess is right—this mountain range is alive. It's a giant clump of life-form readings."

There was a reason why dragon worship was widespread in the Grunade Kingdom.

There was also a reason why monsters wouldn't approach the country.

It's because Grunade took advantage of the fact that monsters wouldn't approach Midgard the Primordial Dragon, and it used an artifact to keep the creature in a deep sleep.

The result was a holy land that would repel all monsters other than dragons where a small town was built, which then grew into a city, then became an entire kingdom.

The reason why whoever exchanged the stone would die was because the moment they replaced the stone, Midgard would wake for a brief moment and kill the individual who replaced it.

As for replacing the artifact's stone, so long as the person possesses a magic device that only the king possesses, it can be done by someone who isn't related by blood to the royal family.

Due to the artifact's very loose restrictions on use, Alice proposed making an irredeemably awful criminal the king temporarily, but—

"Hey, Lydia. Leave the rest to me, the queen. I'm good at hunting giant lizards. I've killed a bunch of lizards since I got to this planet."

"By lizards, do you mean Bursting Lizards? Comparing those to the Primordial Dragon is…"

Lydia can't hide her concern as Belial insists on referring to lesser dragons as lizards.

Belial's in a good mood, having convinced Lydia to temporarily make her queen by arguing she'd at least make sure things worked out okay.

Tiger Man, who has been raising a bit of a fuss, seeing Lydia and Belial's exchange, slumps his shoulders.

"Fine...I'm committing to this, nyeow. I'm gonna spend mrrrost of the Evil Points I have to support you, mrrm."

......

"You're a mutant and a leader. You're standing on the frontlines with me."

"Nyopenyopyopenyopenyope!"

Seeing Tiger Man resume meowing, Lydia looks a bit troubled.

"Um, what do you mean on the frontlines? I thought Lady Belial was going to swap the stone for me..."

Having listened to Lydia's explanation, Belial had very handsomely offered to take care of everything.

Lydia evidently took that to mean Belial would be taking on the task of swapping out the stone.

But if that was all that Belial was planning to do, Tiger Man wouldn't be raising this big of a fuss...

And just then...

"Boss, I brought them as you asked!"

The ones waving their hands as they arrived in the Midgard Mountains were Rose and Russell carrying Nadia between them.

"Mrrm?! What are you doing here, Nyodia? It's dangerous here, you should go hrrrome. Mrr."

"The lizard lady told me I could come watch you being really impressive, Mr. Tiger."

Hearing that, Mr. Tiger glares at me, the one who gave the lizard lady her orders.

"C'mon, Mr. Tiger, Nyodia's watching. Hoping to see just what you can do."

"You better be ready for what's coming your way once this is all done. I'm going to put all sorts of things in my report to Lady Astaroth, mrrr!"

Mr. Tiger puffs out his chest as he tries to threaten me, but in those terms, I have the high ground.

"If I report your crimes from this whole incident, Tiger Man, the retribution squad's going to come looking for you."

"There's nrooo way I'd actually do something like that to mrrry best friend Six! When we get back to Hideout City, I'll take you to a good bar!"

My best friend meows and wraps his arm around my shoulder to play off his last comment as a joke.

"Stop playing around, Tiger Man! Hurry up and commit yourself, dammit!"

Receiving both Belial's chastising and Nadia's hopes, Tiger Man looks up.

"Frrrrine. On mrrry prrride as a mutant, I'll deal with this purrri-mordial dragon or whatever! Mrrrm!"

Alice shakes her head even as Tiger Man declares his readiness.

"Lady Belial, this isn't gonna work. I checked this thing's mass, you won't be able to do anything to it without using a nuke or something. It's impossible to blast apart an entire mountain range without a huge arsenal of weapons. And you don't have your teleporter, Lady Belial. You can't even order weapons right now, right?"

As Alice says, if we're really going to fight an enemy that's the size of the mountain range in front of us, yeah, that doesn't sound doable.

But right now, we've got the most powerful, most tenacious boss in Kisaragi with us.

"Listen to me, Alice. No one in Kisaragi should ever use the word 'impossible.'"

Belial then crosses her arms across her chest and looks up at the Midgard Mountains, stepping out in front of the box-shaped machine that's probably the artifact.

When I look over the rest of the Midgard Mountains, I can see the faint outlines of a dragon.

Meaning the giant life-form several miles long is really about to start moving.

"Mutant Tiger Man, here's your orders! Once Midgard the Primordial Dragon awakes, buy me three minutes of time!"

"Impossible!"

Belial glares at Tiger Man for his immediate rejection of her orders.

"Say that it's impossible again, and I'll give you a beating."

"It's impossible if I don't gigantify."

Tiger Man goes sprawling as Belial follows through on her threat.

"You really punched me! I did say 'if I don't gigantify.' You're always so damned unreasonable, mrr!"

"Well, I mean, you mutants can't use gigantification until you're near death, right?"

I guess that was just Belial trying, in her own way, to help Tiger Man gigantify.

Tiger Man is struck dumb for a moment, but then murmurs out his next sentence as a last gasp of defiance.

"Gigantification heavily consumes a mutant's lifespan, and we're told we should only use it once. But I've already used it twice, mrrrm..."

"I see. Just shut up and do it."

"Totally unreasonable!"

Belial forces Tiger Man to shut up, then turns to me standing toward the back.

"Combat Agent Six! Send a memo to Kisaragi HQ asking for all the nitro cartridges they've got!"

"Seriously? If you take that much nitro, I can't take any responsibility for what happens afterwards."

How in character for Belial to put her own body on the line when she's making her subordinate Tiger Man do the same.

Clasping her arms together over her head, Belial stretches out her back and then begins warm-up exercises.

As I send the order to Kisaragi, I think back to when Belial helped me loosen up my body by stretching with me until the morning.

I guess the Belial from then and the Belial from now are the same at the most basic level.

Although she had been so tame and skittish before her enhancement surgery, she now says…

"Alice! If anything happens to me, explain the situation to Kisaragi HQ! I should have about half a million Evil Points saved up. Say that it's my last command, and as a special exception, have them transfer my points over. Use those points to deal with the Primordial Dragon before it manages to fully wake up!"

She, the person who, since receiving her surgery, has tried more than anyone to protect her allies…

"Half a million points? Are you serious?! Just what did you do, Lady Belial? Well, with that many points and every option on the table, the dragon…should be killable… Would it be? Maybe…?"

…is now fully committed to taking out a monster so big, so powerful, that even challenging it seemed foolhardy, all for the sake of a princess she's just met, a princess of a country that had been an enemy.

"U-um… You can't possibly mean to defeat Midgard? Midgard the monster that's worshipped as a god, and is said to end the world once awakened…?"

Lydia looks up in disbelief, prompting Belial to lightly pat her on the head.

"Once I do, that means you and your descendants won't ever have to risk your lives swapping out stones, right?"

She smiles gently, and Lydia's face flushes as she stands there in shock.

Yeah, even when she's lost her memories, she's still the same person at heart.

So unabashedly generous, the sheltered girl, who would have lived quietly and calmly had the world been peaceful, turns her back to Lydia and calls out loudly:

"Step forward once the artifact's sorcery stone is removed, Mutant Loli-man! But before we do that, call out your crimes that caused this whole incident!"

"I abandoned my post of defending the hideout, then kidnapped a princess who was still a minor and stole a national treasure! I assaulted knights who invaded the woodlands, and committed countless violations of orders by interfering with the invasion plans of Alice and the others, and increased the ranks of enemy countries, mrrrm!"

You can't deny the man is pretty bad when he's got a list of crimes like that.

It's not an exaggeration to say this entire affair is all his fault.

"Ordinarily, execution is a fitting penalty for all of that, but if you survive this encounter, you're absolved of all of your recent screwups! Your beloved lolis are behind you. Don't you dare back down, even if it kills you!"

"Hrmph. You may be an unreasonable, violent, and toxic boss, but you're always so damned good at motivating us to frrright!"

Belial knocks the sorcery stone from its place on the artifact.

As everyone waits, something toward the bottom of the mountain range opens.

Based on the fact that it seemed to move to focus on something, that must be Midgard opening its eye.

Standing in front of the artifact, Belial wobbles for a moment when that eye stares at her.

Watching from a distance, Rose yells out at the top of her lungs:

"Lady Belial, that's no ordinary eye! It's an evil eye that can kill the weak-willed with a single gaze, so please be careful!"

Having heard words that sound like something out of a cringy eighth grader's notebook, Tiger Man steps forward as if to protect Belial.

We can feel Midgard awakening as the ground below us begins to shake.

Two of Earth's greatest beasts face off against a life-form far beyond the size of any reasonable scale, one the size of an entire mountain range.

Russell looks at their backs like a child looking at the hero he admires and calls over.

"Don't you dare lose, Tiger Man! You're the ultimate mutant, aren't you?!"

"Tiger Man! Lady Belial! If you need help, call! I can at least buy you two seconds by really, really trying!"

I really don't think she could last that long, but Rose, drawn in by the two of them, offers her cheers, holding her fist up.

The ground shakes so much that we can't remain standing, and Lydia takes her little sister's hand and kneels as though in prayer.

"Super-giant hostile life-form, Midgard the Primordial Dragon. If we can kill this thing and send its samples back to Earth, it'll be a gigantic profit!"

Even Alice the android seems to be infected by the heat of the moment and urges them on.

"Lady Belial, here comes the nitro cartridges! The rest is up to you!"

Belial, who has been waiting behind Tiger Man with her arms crossed, injects the just-arrived nitro cartridges into her neck without a moment's hesitation.

"Mr. Tiger! Go get 'em!"

Nadia, evidently feeling something in the air, adds her own voice to the fray.

Tiger Man's broad back twitches, and the Midgard Mountains slowly begin to move.

When the Primordial Dragon turns its body, the rocks that had been deposited upon its body begin to rain down like avalanches, but they're all blasted to pieces by Belial's giant explosion!

"I am Tiger Man, King of the Woodlands and leader in the Kisaragi Corporation! So long as I have the cheers of the lolis behind me, dragons don't scare mreee!"

"I, Belial of the Hellfire, Supreme Leader of Kisaragi Corporation, have come from a distant world to hunt all the hostile life-forms and invade this planet!"

With a thunderous cacophony like a volcanic explosion, the giant mountain range flings off the earth and rock that was crusted onto its body, giving a great roar as it rears up!

In terms of time, the fight lasted all of three minutes.

However…

"Everything's been completely blasted away…"

Rose murmurs in a shocked stupor, but no one responds.

No, it's probably more accurate to say no one can reply.

"That was more than I imagined. I didn't think it would be this much."

The one who finally voices some agreement is Alice, the only one here who's spotless, thanks to hiding behind me.

By "more than she imagined," does she mean the legendary monster Midgard or Belial's combat ability that managed to defeat even that monster?

"Forget that. You need to stop hiding behind me every time something happens."

"Aw, don't be like that, partner. You know if I take damage, the whole neighborhood's gonna have a bad day," Alice says before she starts gently wiping the dirt off my face with a towel, but that's definitely not enough to fool me.

I take another look around, but thanks to the Primordial Dragon Midgard's rampage, there's nothing there.

The trees that had been growing in scattered clumps and the smaller mountains were blasted away.

And on this ground, which has been reduced to nothing but a giant empty space, lies the giant body of Midgard itself. Lydia, having confirmed that it's stopped moving, stares up at it in shock.

Even as I stand there having trouble accepting what's just happened, Belial appears covered in dirt. It seems she must have broken her right arm, hanging limply by her side. She calls out to me:

"Six! Ready a bath!"

I hand a moist towel to my unreasonable boss, who demands the comforts of civilization out here in the middle of nowhere.

"We'll have to wait until we get back to the hideout. Besides, if you take a bath in a place like this, I'll be guaranteed to peek. I might even come and join you in the bath."

"Well, that's another thing to add to my report. Go and get chewed out by Astaroth."

Alice injects Belial's broken arm with medical nanobots as we banter, and nearby, a badly wounded Tiger Man smirks with a pale, deathly expression as he's taken care of by two lolis.

And—

"For them to actually take down the Primordial Dragon…"

Lydia murmurs in shock, staring up at the sprawling body of Midgard.

A bright-eyed Rose climbs atop Midgard's corpse and begins gnawing on it.

"Good thing microwaving did the trick! If that didn't work, we would've had to order a shipment of nukes!"

"That's definitely not an order I'd let you place. Well, in any case, well done."

What Belial calls microwaving is a name Lilith gave to a move spawned from pyrokinesis.

From what they told me, it works by directly heating a life-form's cells instead of attacking them with flames. It's basically a finisher that works like the heating mechanism in a microwave.

Because it looks grotesque when used on living creatures, it's a big move that Belial doesn't like to use much.

When Midgard awoke, it first took aim at Tiger Man.

Having already been badly injured when Belial hit him, he didn't hesitate to use his trump card, burning his own lifespan to gigantify and grab Midgard's head.

Belial climbed onto the rampaging dragon's head, then used all of the available nitro cartridges to nuke its brain, leading us to our current situation.

After she finishes wiping the dirt off her face, Belial starts walking to Lydia, who's dumbstruck.

The princess, seeing the raw power wielded just moments ago, trembles and is unable to move.

Everyone stops what they're doing to watch as Belial approaches the princess.

As we watch with our breath held to hear what unreasonable, impossible demand Belial will make for this act of stupendous achievement…

"Hey, Lydia. As you can see, I've killed the Primordial Dragon that's been causing you so much heartache."

Lydia's caught in dumbfounded awe as Belial makes it sound like she hasn't done anything of real consequence.

"Y-yes! Um, to receive such a blessing, and to have been shown that level of power, our kingdom will happily pay whatever amount that you choose to ask for—"

Belial grins from ear to ear, cutting off Lydia with a laugh.

"Can we call it even for all the crap Tiger Man caused, like stealing the national treasure, kidnapping, and all the rest?"

At the unexpected words, Lydia looks at Belial as though she can't believe her eyes.

Then, looking upon Belial as though she were a hero who arrived when all hope was lost and saved the day:

"...Y-yes. Yes, of course!"

Lydia smiles brightly, an expression of pure joy appropriate for someone her age, a smile unburdened by the constant tension that was, until then, a fixed feature on her face.

7

"Whaaaaaaaaaaaaat?! Y-y-y-you slew M-M-M-Midgard?!"

When we return to the palace in triumph, Adelie greets us with an expression of utter disbelief.

"Yep. I'm told it's the thing responsible for killing generations of kings in this country. So we've solved the problem for good."

Adelie's shifty-eyed confusion says everything we need to know about just how remarkable Belial's achievement is.

"What were you doing, then? Did you know that someone had to die every time the stones were replaced? You're supposed to be a hero; isn't killing that thing your responsibility?"

"What are you talking about?! You told me to look after Princess Nadia! I was playing with her in the castle when the chimera came to pick her up, so...! Besides, Midgard isn't supposed to be something people can kill!"

Oh, she's been making herself useful in looking after Nadia, I guess.

"Even we'd avoided dealing with it directly, trying to manage it from a distance... W-what should I do? The death of the Primordial

Dragon is going to have an incalculable impact on the world! ...I—I need to get going..."

Adelie looks dazed as she murmurs some tantalizing information while wandering out of the room, but she's not the priority right now.

We're currently inside the throne room—

"Lydia, can you at least explain what's going on?! Why was Midgard slain?! I thought you went to change out the sorcery stone!"

The princess, looking relieved now that the problem has been taken care of, is being interrogated by the prince.

"I'm saying that now that my objective is complete, I'm handing you the throne. Sometimes you're just a little too sentimental, so make sure you fix that... If you have a cynical person among your retinue, you should make them one of your close advisors."

Seems the prince doesn't know that the person exchanging the sorcery stone usually dies in the process.

And this *tsundere* princess doesn't seem inclined to explain something that's no longer an issue.

"Lydia! Do you really think you can throw the country into a whirlwind of confusion and just walk off the stage like that? And I have no cynical people in my retinue! The most cynical person in this kingdom is, without a doubt, you, my sister!"

She chuckles softly at Madia's string of insults, then shrugs.

"Then, in exchange for giving you the throne, will you make me your chancellor?"

"Pardon...?!"

Lydia smiles in amusement, her teasing tone clearly enough to...

"...Lydia, are you serious about abdicating your claim?"

...tell the prince that she isn't kidding.

The prince looks troubled and confused as he turns to face us.

"Even if I asked you what happened, I'm sure you wouldn't tell me, would you?"

No, I don't have any objection to just blabbing, but...

Well, the *tsundere* princess is putting her index finger to her lips with a smile, so I guess the nicest thing to do here is to say nothing.

As we stay quiet, Lydia gives us a weary smile.

"We now owe a lot to Kisaragi's people. Our kingdom will be facing a great deal of challenges from here on out. After all, we no longer have the benefits of our proximity to Midgard. Like other lands, monsters will come back to our territories."

"Yes, what a terrible headache this will be. What are we to do…?"

As the prince cradles his head with a troubled expression, Lydia chuckles.

"In the grand scheme of things, it's not such a serious matter. It would have been one thing if this were back when the kingdom was founded, but with our current resources, we should be able to handle it. It's not like the time of our ancestors, who wandered the land looking for a safe place to call home. Thanks to their efforts and those of succeeding generations, we now have strong walls and skilled soldiers…"

Lydia smiles as though a great burden has been lifted from her shoulders.

"There's no need to worry about monsters. I'm here, after all."

At Belial's remark, Alice lets out a sigh of admiration.

As I sit there hoping for an explanation.

"You know our line of work, right, Princess Lydia? What Lady Belial's trying to say is this," Alice says, then nudges me with her elbow, which instantly clues me into what she's trying to say.

I repeat the words I once said to the Grace Kingdom.

"What Lady Belial is trying to say is this: Care to hire some Combat Agents?"

Lydia breaks into a happy smile at that remark, and the prince lets out a sigh of resignation and shrugs.

"Nope. Why are you trying to look cool? I'm saying I'm going to stay in this kingdom."

Belial, not even bothering to read the room, starts going off on a ridiculous tangent again.

Having had my cool line ruined by Belial's remark, I offer my objection.

"So what DID you mean, then? Don't say you're going to stay here as an advisor or guest!" I say, rather more harshly than needed, trying to hide my embarrassment.

"Why would I bother being a guest? I'm already the queen, aren't I?" Belial asks, ridiculously, as though this were the simplest thing in the world.

As I'm trying to figure out how to knock this childish leader down a peg:

"......That's true, Lady Belial hasn't returned the throne even after exchanging the sorcery stone," Alice says almost to herself, resulting in Lydia and the prince both freezing in shock.

"...U-um, Lady Belial? Even as a joke, it's a bit in poor taste, is it not? Lady Belial, you're the hero who defeated Midgard to save us, aren't you?"

"Hiyah!"

"Oww!"

"Lydia?!"

Belial suddenly slaps Lydia's cheek at that question.

"What a terrible thing to suddenly do! Poor Princess Lydia's all crying now!"

But Belial puffs out her chest as though to tell me that I'm wrong.

"You're such a dummy, Six. Do you not know the whole thing about sticks and carrots? That was a stick for pretty much blackmailing you guys into working. It's extracting a cost as an evil corporation."

"Um, considering how much trouble Tiger Man caused, I think it would've been fine to just provide Princess Lydia with carrots. Also, be honest, you slapped her because she called you a hero, didn't you?"

It's true that an evil corporation relies on its reputation, and that it's important to make sure no one gets away with disrespecting it, but I wish she'd at least read the room a bit.

"L-Lydia, are you all right?! Why did you hire these ruffians...?"

Lydia holds back tears for a moment from the pain of Belial's slap, but she's evidently amused at the fact that her brother, who was her enemy just a few hours ago, is worried about her, and she begins to chuckle.

"See? Look at her, the stick worked, didn't it?"

"No, I think she's just a masochist."

"I don't have such predilections! I just couldn't help but chuckle because of the circumstances!"

Lydia then clears her throat and straightens her dress.

"Yes, you're correct, I hadn't properly apologized to Kisaragi yet. I apologize that, in my desperation, I used such awful methods to force you to work for me. But thanks to your help, my brother's come around... I really do need to thank you."

"Lydia! ...You seriously owe me an explanation later for suddenly giving up on the throne you were so fixated on, and with everything that happened with them."

The prince, who looked so troubled by the events unfolding in the throne room, then turns to Lydia and offers her a weary smile.

"Hiyah!"

"Guh?!"

"Madia?!

I guess Belial really doesn't like reading the room, because she slaps the prince this time.

"You really can't go around just doing that, Lady Belial. Now what upset you?"

"The fact that they're trying to bring this whole thing to a close like it's a beautiful, touching ending. I told you, I'm the queen... But, well, I guess I'll give you the throne back, but in exchange, you're going to become a vassal of Kisaragi. Make sure you pay your tribute."

"W-wait, why would we ever listen to a demand like that?! Just who are you people?! You suddenly come in and cause all sorts of problems, then demand that we pay tribute?! Our country, the Grunade Kingdom, is a great power with a proud history! This is going too far!"

What the prince is saying is perfectly reasonable, but logic has no place when dealing with Belial.

"Proud history?! There's nothing to be proud of, given it's a history built on the sacrifices of people. Countries like that deserve to be destroyed. Hell, I'll go and destroy them myself. After all, I'm a Supreme Leader in an evil corporation!"

"Wha...?!"

Belial smirks maliciously, prompting a stunned silence from the prince.

Despite the frightening statement from Belial, Lydia begins to chuckle.

"Vassalage, mm? Since you hold the throne, I suppose we have no choice. That, and if you really wanted to, you could easily destroy us, Lady Belial."

"Well, vassalage isn't all bad, you know. If you're ever in trouble, just call us. It doesn't matter how far away I am, whether it's another continent or even another planet, I swear I'll come and save you."

Belial suddenly looks and sounds the part of a white knight, and Lydia blushes.

The thing about Belial is that even when she seems so unreasonable, she has that innate charisma to suck people onto her side.

"All right, guess I should give you a carrot to go with that stick."

Belial then presses an object into the hesitant Lydia's hand.

"This is a tool called a digital voice recorder. When I go home, press the button here that says 'play.' Also, make sure you press that when all three of you siblings are in the same room."

The prince tilts his head quizzically at Belial and Lydia's exchange.

"Once you all listen to this recording together, question your little sister as to why she asked the Tiger Man, who came to steal the national treasure, to kidnap her as well."

As I watch Belial say all of this with a malicious grin, I think about what's probably contained in that voice recorder.

8

"And so after all the complications, we managed to elegantly defeat Midgard the Primordial Dragon, solved the problem that a princess had been grappling with on her own, and made Grunade submit to us."

It's been a week since we returned from the Grunade Kingdom.

Having taken the time to recover from our journey, I've found refuge in Viper's office to avoid my boss's daily barrage of unreasonable demands.

Viper pauses her pen and smiles gently over to me.

"Well, it sounds like you made quite the impact. Everyone's already talking about how you and the others defeated Midgard."

Alice smirks as she processes her own paperwork.

"Thanks to that, I think we can rest assured that the countries and city-states that submitted to us will stay loyal. Seems Midgard was a really famous monster around the continent, and we've had a constant stream of well-wishers. Even the cities and villages that had been on the fence have come to ask for our protection."

Thanks to Belial's rampage, we've dramatically expanded our influence, and our name's become famous throughout the lands.

In the end, everything turns out for the best. Could it be that Belial did everything knowing this would be the outcome?

"Um… That reminds me, Mr. Six. Do you know where Heine went? I haven't seen her for days…"

"Oh, we left Heine with Snow in Grunade. I'm sure they'll eventually work out their differences and come home."

"W-why would you leave them there? W-well, so long as they come back safely, it should be fine..."

There'd been continued tension between them since their little dust-up, so we decided to force them to get back to Grace on their own.

Nothing builds friendships like shared struggles.

For the sake of having one less complication, I'd rather that those two become friends again.

Just then:

"Hey, Six, get over here! Alice works, too! Help me!"

Our peaceful little day is shattered as Belial's voice thunders out from the direction of the training grounds.

Alice and I exchange glances and head over to find Belial trying to disentangle from Grimm, who's clinging needily to Belial's waist.

"This is your underling, right?! Do something! She's a serious nuisance!"

Belial had looked like death from the side effects of using all those nitro cartridges, but after a couple days, she'd gotten over her nitro hangover, and her broken arm from fighting Midgard had healed cleanly, leaving her to interact with the local hires, but—

"Everyone's so mean to me! Why? Why do I always get forgotten?! How many times has it been that I wake up and everything's finished?! Come on, take me with you already!"

"You need to be complaining to Six, not me! We had no choice, you were dead!"

Grimm, who had died because Belial had forced her to wear socks, is throwing a tantrum.

"That's exactly it! You killed me, why are you so cold to me?! Lady Belial, you're a Supreme Leader, so you're like a mother-in-law to me, aren't you?!"

"Nope."

Belial flatly rejects that argument, but Grimm clings on with a tenacity unique to the undead.

"Besides, you were supposed to be dead. What are you doing getting back up? From now on, you can call yourself the Mutant Zombie Woman."

"N-no, that title's not cute at all! Let's see… If you're going to give me a title, why not make it sound all shimmery and cute like something to do with being a saint…?"

Belial quirks her finger to summon me over after she shoves the zombie woman and dreamily contemplates alternative titles for her.

"Six, get me some steel wire. I'll tie her up and leave her lying around to keep her out of my hair."

"D-don't! I'm pretty vulnerable to being physically restrained like that! I understand! I won't complain anymore! So please…"

I tie up Grimm using the steel wire I ordered, and Belial gags her to silence her. Belial then gestures for me to follow her.

I leave Grimm tied up on the training field and follow Belial, ending up in the teleportation room.

Wait, she's not thinking of heading back to Earth right as she's finished healing, is she?

"Are you going back already? I mean, Tiger Man is still recuperating in the hospital, so you're more than justified in staying awhile longer, Lady Belial. You can be like Lady Lilith and spend a little time slacking off here! Let's enjoy life for a little bit."

"Don't compare me to Lilith, I can't slack off now that my body's finished healing. That, and I've already been summoned back to Earth. The cricket-type superheroes, who are enough of a pain on their own, are evidently looking at forming some teams. That's a lot to deal with, even for me."

Well, yeah, that's a seriously bad situation.

How bad? Honestly, it makes Midgard seem like a small inconvenience by comparison.

Still...

"Why do you always play hard to get, Lady Belial? This is the first time I've seen you in ages, but we've been so busy, we didn't even get to properly sit down and have a chat. Why don't you just stay here? I'd love to actually be able to go out and enjoy this world with you."

When I can't help but say what I really feel, Belial looks at me, her expression torn.

"...You know, you really are a natural charmer. I bet you said something like that to Lilith, too. She was all happy when she got back to Earth."

"You're the charmer, Lady Belial. I didn't say anything of the sort to Lady Lilith. I didn't try to stop her when she left."

I mean, I couldn't see Lilith being all that useful even if she had stayed behind.

If anything, she probably would've been all sorts of a pain in the ass, what with how needy she can be.

Belial smiles softly, evidently sensing what I'm thinking.

"Got it. Well, you and Lilith are more like brother and sister than anything else...but that's the sort of line you should be saying to Astaroth, not me."

"If I ever said something like that to Lady Astaroth, she'd get mad at me, telling me to stop being such an idiot and get back to work. As it is, she already seems to be in a bad mood whenever I see her face over video chat."

Belial furrows her brow, a mix of emotions playing out on her face.

"...Astaroth's pretty socially clumsy, but you're almost as bad."

She then holds her collar closed for a moment, letting out a slow breath.

Belial's face suddenly takes on a serious expression, and she straightens, before calling out:

"Here are your orders!"

At Belial's announcement, Alice and I stand at attention.

"This time, we've been able to greatly expand Kisaragi's influence. But we're still far too short on land. A message from Astaroth: The Earth has little time left. Speed up the invasion."

What do you mean, Earth has little time left? Why do you people always leave me hanging with these interesting statements?

Then again, if I learn more, I'm pretty sure I'd have nowhere to run to, so for now, I'm happier staying ignorant.

Belial smiles softly as if reading my thoughts from my expression.

"Don't worry about how things are going over there. You just need to work hard, but not risk your lives. For the sake of Tiger Man's sacrifice, make sure you guys stay alive."

"Tiger Man's just recuperating in the infirmary! Why are you so eager to kill him?"

Tiger Man, despite his third gigantification, managed to cling to life, and he's been sleeping off his injuries as Rose and Russell look after him.

Alice says he should wake up soon, but since we brought him home without saying goodbye to Princess Nadia, you can bet there'll be a hassle or two to deal with when he wakes up.

Belial puts her hands on Alice's and my head and roughly tussles our hair.

"See ya, guys. It wasn't long, but it was pretty fun. Since I gotta make some preparations to face the cricket supes, I'm gonna head off now."

"You did whatever you felt like doing and it was only 'pretty' fun? C'mon, Lady Belial, you need to let your hair down a little. Why are you always living your life in a hurry? Don't make us worry about you so much."

At my question, Belial seems about to speak, forcing a troubled smile to her lips.

"...Well, there she goes. I was hoping we could spend time like we used to, go out partying, maybe engage in a little cuddling...but I guess Lady Belial's always been hard to get."

In the end, Belial didn't say anything before stepping into the teleporter and heading home without another word.

"...That's how it looked like to you, eh? Well, I'm thinking Lady Belial knew that there'd be trouble if she stayed any longer."

"Yeah, she did mention that the cricket superheroes are about to form teams. 'Trouble' is not a strong enough word for that."

As I worry about everyone back on Earth, Alice looks like she has something she wants to say.

"That's not the kind of trouble I meant, but, well, that's fine... Now, Six, have you noticed?"

"...? Noticed what?"

Alice gazes at the now empty teleporter.

"Based on the fact that she ultimately managed to greatly expand our territory and solved the drama between the Grunade royals...I'm pretty sure Lady Belial's gotten some of her memories back."

[Intermission 5] —And So I Head Off-World—

"What's wrong, Belial? Don't suddenly start crying like that—you scared me for a minute there! Did you remember something important?"

As my vision blurs from the tears, I see Lilith panicking.

I slowly sit up and look around. I can see that I'm in Lilith's lab.

"No, it's not that I remembered..."

It feels like I've been in a very long dream.

Astaroth created the Kisaragi Corporation, then he and Lilith joined up.

There was a lot that didn't go right at first, but the corporation started to grow.

Of course, we made a lot of enemies in the process, but we made a lot more allies in the process.

I thought things would keep going well.

As he and Astaroth went from constantly fighting to getting closer, I found myself torn between being happy and being sad.

Astaroth is my best friend, so I was happy she was getting to like him.

He's also a dear friend, so it was hard to watch him getting closer to Astaroth.

I hated the fact that I was so weak that I had to lie to myself, afraid to damage our current, comfortable friendship, despite the fact that I knew full well why I felt such pain in my chest.

Still, it was so fun to be with everyone that I wanted things to keep going that way forever.

Things would probably have stayed that way if he hadn't been seriously injured fighting the superheroes.

When I saw him sleeping after receiving enhancement surgery, I made the decision to undergo surgery as well.

"Hey, Belial, we can stop if it's painful. There's no need to force yourself to remember."

I want the power to protect everyone. I want to be someone with the exact opposite personality, someone strong, someone everyone can depend on.

Lilith explained to me that the more of my brain I dedicated to my abilities, the stronger my abilities would become.

And so, after Lilith set the dial to the very limit of what was safe, I turned the dial myself and—

"Oh."

"...? What is it? Are your memories okay?"

......Have I become a strong person?

I know I have the greatest power of anyone in Kisaragi when it comes to fighting, but I don't think my heart is all that strong yet.

I'm going to go see him again. And if I feel like I've really become strong, then—

"Hey, what do you mean 'oh'?! Hey, Belial, don't ignore me!"

Epilogue

Belial smiles as Astaroth and Lilith wait for her in front of the teleporter.

"Hey, I'm home!"

"Took you long enough! It's been a mess over here. Somehow the superheroes got wind that you were away and staged a huge counteroffensive."

Lilith snarks at Belial's laid-back greeting.

"We tried contacting you, but the teleporter wasn't working properly. Then when we tried calling Hideout City, but they said you'd gotten lost. And when we finally figured out where you were, we get the news you got hurt and needed to stay there awhile. Just what the heck were you fighting over there?!"

"Six and I went after this ginormous dragon called the Primordial. I brought back a sample as a souvenir, so do what you want with it."

For some reason, Lilith freezes at Belial's words.

"O-oh? You went hunting with him like in *MonPan*…? And a dragon to boot?!"

"Yeah, I also got to rough up a bunch of other monsters. Got to beat back some barbarians and forced a few neighboring countries to bend the knee, too. The details are all in the report."

"'Bunch of other monsters…'" As Lilith mutters darkly to herself, Astaroth smiles gently at Belial.

"I'm so glad you're back. It really is like you to get things done even when you end up getting lost."

"Hey! W-wait, that makes me sound like I'm useless!" Lilith says in shock.

"Six was telling me how you spent all your time there playing around. He even said he didn't bother trying to keep you there when you left."

"That son of a…! Get off the teleporter, Belial! I'm going to go give him a piece of my—"

Astaroth grabs Lilith by the collar of her lab coat as she tries to barge into the teleporter.

"Not while the cricket heroes are gathering at our doorstep."

"I won't be long. I just need to give him a beating."

Lilith slips out of Astaroth's grasp by sliding out of her lab coat, but Belial intercepts her before she can get into the teleporter.

"There's no way you'd come back if we let you go. You just want to slack off until we've beaten back the capes."

"Of course not! You make it sound like I'm afraid of the superheroes! I'm just pissed off Six went off hunting with you, a non-gamer. I wanna go hunting, too!"

"Go hunt superheroes before you go hunting dragons. If I'm honest, I want to go over there, too…"

Astaroth sighs, prompting a smirk from Lilith.

"Oh, so that's why you've been in a bad mood lately. If you want to see Six so badly, you should go visit."

"I can't go visit Six while my subordinates are fighting heroes… …Ahem, I have no idea what you're talking about. Hurry up and prepare for battle."

Astaroth purses her lips and nudges Lilith. Belial snaps her fingers as though the exchange jogged something in her mind.

"That reminds me, Six was worried that he'd upset you, Astaroth. At least try to be nicer to him when you're video-chatting with him. If you're not careful, one of the locals'll end up taking him."

"Wha?! He really said that?! A-all right. I suppose it's part of my job to motivate the Combat Agents, so I guess..."

Perhaps pleased with the fact that Six observed her that carefully during their occasional chats, Astaroth un-purses her lips and almost cracks a smile.

Belial's expression is clouded as she watches Astaroth, but then she adds:

"...Yeah, you better. Else Six is gonna try to sweet-talk me into staying by telling me he wants to spend more time with me or that I should chill out and live there with them."

""?!""

Astaroth and Lilith freeze at her sudden bombshell revelation.

"You mentioned he didn't even bother trying to get me to stay when I left..."

Astaroth's brow twitches at Lilith's muttering...

"Superhero Alert! Superhero Alert! The cricket superheroes have finished gathering and are moving to attack! Mutants and Supreme Leaders, please prepare to defend against them!"

The klaxon blares within Kisaragi Headquarters, warning of an impending superhero attack.

In response, Belial sets down the pack she was carrying and begins stretching her shoulders.

Lilith turns to Belial and says:

"There's something different about you lately, Belial. You're not as airheaded as you used to be, but it's hard to put a finger on it. Did something happen while you were over there? You kind of looked refreshed when you came back."

Belial finishes stretching and turns to Lilith.

"Well, I did get seriously injured over there. Maybe the shock brought my memories back."

She smiles teasingly, then dashes off to intercept the oncoming heroes.

"Now's not the time; let's get going, Lilith!"

"H-hey! Aren't you at least a little curious?! She said her memories might have returned! Something happened over there! Something involving Six!"

As they chase after Belial, Astaroth responds.

"Of course I'm curious! But we need to deal with the superheroes first! Then we'll sit her down and question her properly!"

"Uh, Astaroth, you're scaring me! That's why Six thinks you're mad at him!"

Listening to their banter, Belial arches her lips into a joyful smile and charges headlong into the oncoming rush of superheroes!

AFTERWORD

Thank you for picking up Volume 7 of *Combatants Will be Dispatched!* It is I, the author, Natsume Akatsuki.

This is the first new volume in a while.

How long is a while? Well, the last volume came out over a year and a half ago.

I swear it's not because the author's been lazy. I've been busy writing special bonus stories for the disc release of *Combatants* and serving as a consulting producer, doing all sorts of things other than writing books.

Yes, discs.

In the time since the last volume, the *Combatants* anime ran on the air!

I've been involved with anime adaptations for a while now, but it's still not something that comes naturally for me.

Despite all the problems with production during the COVID pandemic, the anime staff have done a wonderful job. I can definitely recommend it to those who are interested.

Now, as for this volume, as you can see from the cover, it's a Belial-focused volume.

She's the Supreme Leader who, though born and raised as the proper daughter of an established family, ended up with a completely different personality due to her modification surgery.

She hasn't quite gotten all of her memories and personality back, but things are looking promising.

There's still quite a bit of mystery surrounding Belial that's part of her background story. There's actually a reason why she's a bit of a workaholic, and I think that'll be revealed in due time.

Lilith, on the other hand, has always just been that way, and I doubt she's going to change much in the future.

She'll probably keep snacking on potato chips and reading manga or playing video games and working when she feels like it.

Our heroes ran into the Primordial Dragon in this volume. Turns out the Primordial Dragon's like a secret RPG boss monster that only shows up in the second playthrough.

So what'll happen to the world now that it's been defeated? Hopefully I'll get to explore this in the coming volumes.

Speaking of which, this was a volume where I blew past deadlines again and again and caused lots of problems for a lot of people.

I feel like I spend every afterword apologizing, but somehow we crossed the finish line thanks to the work of Kakao Lanthanum, my project managers, the designers, my editors, the salespeople, and the other people involved in the production of this volume.

As I close out this afterword, I'd like to express my thanks and sincere apologies to everyone involved in this book and…

Finally, a big, big thanks to all the readers who've picked up this book and continue to support this series!

Natsume Akatsuki